Boulevard Wren and Other Stories

Boulevard Wren and Other Stories

Blindboy Boatclub

GILL BOOKS

Gill Books
Hume Avenue
Park West
Dublin 12
www.gillbooks.ie

Gill Books is an imprint of M.H. Gill & Co.

© Blindboy Boatclub 2019

978 07171 83334 0

Copy-edited by Emma Dunne
Designed by www.grahamthew.com
Printed by CPI Group (UK) Ltd, Croydon CRO 4YY

This book is typeset in 10.5 on 15pt, Sabon.

The paper used in this book comes from the wood pulp of
managed forests. For every tree felled, at least one tree is
planted, thereby renewing natural resources.
A CIP catalogue record for this book is available from the
British Library.

5 4 3 2 1

Praise for *The Gospel According to Blindboy*

'Mad, wild, hysterical, and all completely under the writer's control – this is a brilliant debut.'
KEVIN BARRY

'There is genius in this book, warped genius. Like you'd expect from a man who for his day job wears a plastic bag on his head but something beyond that too. Oddly in keeping with the tradition of great Irish writers.'
RUSSELL BRAND

'One of Ireland's finest and most intelligent comic minds delivers stories so blisteringly funny and sharp your fingers might bleed. In language so delicious you can taste it, we're shown holy and unholy Ireland: a land of lock-ins, nettle stings, stone-mad Cork birds, gas cunts and Guiney's jeans. No one is safe – we all have the unmerciful piss ripped out of us and there's no escape from the emotional gut punches, expertly dealt.'
TARA FLYNN

'If you've ever witnessed (there's no other word for it) a Rubberbandits video you'll be anxious (there's no other word for it) to read this collection of short stories from one of the originators. I hesitate to use the word author as the experience is as close to reading a traditional short story as being burnt by a blow torch. Essential, funny and disturbing.'
DANNY BOYLE

'Demented, dishevelled and deeply surreal – Blindboy Boatclub's book will shock and delight.'
IRISH INDEPENDENT

'It's not for the faint-hearted.'
JOE.IE

'You won't be disappointed. It will take you to places unexpected.'
RYAN TUBRIDY

* * * * *
SUNDAY BUSINESS POST BOOK OF THE YEAR

Acknowledgements

Helbo, Shontin, Jeff, Nack, Bop, Gad, Phile, Deag, Mr Chrome, DJ Willie O Dea J, Charlie, Cheesy

Contents

BOULEVARD WREN

Lorcan Dooly will only usually sleep in his darkened box-room five storeys up. There is no bed. There's a plastic lounge chair. Recently he's been sleeping outside.

He is wearing a horizontal peach band of late evening sun across his nose. Black slits of pupils reduce under the glare when his irises expand outwards in reptilian clouds. He is forcing his eyelids open. A new vein appears in his neck. It is baby blue and runs up from his shoulder blades to the base of his jaw. Above is an aching mouth, agape, full of false acrylic teeth, pearlescent with glints of mucosal enamel edges. Nostrils curl to sneeze. His open throat makes little bubbly sounds. Then the sunlight passes and his skin is grey again.

His jaw relaxes. The concrete path in front of his eyes looks starry as he slumps alone in the passenger seat of the Flapmagnet down Fintan's Lane, dazzled a bit. He counts the floating objects that slide across his path of vision. He wonders about how they look – like magnified bacteria he once saw in a documentary about germs. He is concerned that the floaters will ruin his dream.

There's a wind outside the car that would strip skin off you. The ears pick up on its whistle and he uses that to focus himself back on the memory of the sunlight.

It's been this way every evening now, 8.10 p.m., with the streak of good weather that's blessed the place. He's been trying his best to dream in the magic hour, that perfect moment of golden evening warmth where everything feels like love. The best dreams are dreamt in the magic hour, vibrating passages with vulgar yellows that make skies purple from lens flares. But Lorcan's dreams are mostly overcast. Greens become an ashy dull silver. Bricks are a flaccid brown. A hazy monotonous glut with no definition around the edges. No feeling in the gut.

So Lorcan tilts his neck back and uses long crinkly fingers to pinch down between his eyes. His forehead pulses tense from trying to memorise the evening sunlight. With a steady hand, he feels his way up his chest and retrieves the zolpidem pill that's been resting in his shirt pocket. It is placed in his mouth. His eyes are fixed on nothing in particular, cradling the exclusive memory of that peachy bronze glare of magic light which dazzled into his brain, holding firmly the internal sensation of contentment that orange sunlight gives upon his belly. The Chinese zolpidem acts fast. His Slumbo device is fully charged on his wrist, and the phone is too. His eyelids have hammers hanging off them. The darkening road and houses drool into themselves with the sleeping pill drizzle.

He is asleep in the front seat, the vintage white Nike cap resting at a forty-five-degree angle on his skull. Inside the car it is dark except for the pulsing LED light of the Slumbo, which inhales and exhales a citrus-green glow from his wrist. It plays on the shapes of his face. It blinks three times and turns purple when Lorcan enters REM sleep. The phone lights up momentarily as the Slumbo app begins to monitor the pulses of the veins in his arm. The car's interior is bathed in the LED glow. The light is a steady, rhythmic calm purple lung.

The Flapmagnet is a faded red 1996 Honda Civic jalopy that was a hand-me-down from the dead brother, Eugene Dooly. Eugene who died when Lorcan was a kid. It is Lorcan's now. It stands on blocks down Fintan's Lane, to the back of his room, no wheels. It's the only car there that could still be called a car and not just a decommissioned petrol vehicle serving as a domicile. It is covered with a tarp when Lorcan's not in it, safe from the winds. On the darkened back window is a vinyl decal that spells out FLAPMAGNET, along with Eugene's old 085 mobile number. Fine motor, one of the last of its kind in Limerick city. Peacock spoilers on the back, low to the ground. The bonnet is a quare matt pink from several summers of salt air below in Kilkee. Inside it welches of cigarette ghosts from a rusted-out ash tray. The fixtures on the dash have that grey injection-moulded plastic pockmark texture that smooths around the doors where decades of bowld hands have touched it. The worn-away rubber cover of the gearstick exposes its geriatric metal, which makes your hands smell like iron when they're on the wheel. It was a coveted boy-racer Civic that made the ould wans of Limerick long to be seen in the front seat, window down, Tiesto blaring. The Flapmagnet is now an antique chariot of shame. You'd need the right carbon permit to even turn the key in the ignition, and it'd cost a few quid for that, even then. The running engine is only for show – usually at a designated meet-up of ould racer heads once a year when the wheels are on, the manky petrol engine announcing itself with foul plumes and roaring the way that electric transport doesn't, ould lads cheering on with a nationalistic pride, remembering things before the collapse. Lorcan wouldn't dare give it road in Limerick or the guards would be involved.

The sun is dead and gone. Outside the car is wearing black. The phone beeps. Lorcan jolts awake with an urgency on him and grabs it in both hands. The app informs him that his Slumbo is rendering. He leaves the seat of the Flapmagnet and sits on its bonnet in the hopes of getting better reception to speed up the progress bar.

Scunter and Boulevard Wren mangle out of a shadow at the back of Fintan's Lane. They move towards the rear of the Flapmagnet, the nephews of Deccy Wren, a big fat tomcat of a man. The two of them come down from the Metal Nest, the Wren clan's walled encampment, which is cut into a crossroads where several lanes converge. There's no escaping the Wrens. Sharp figures with a pair of vicious heads on them pointed at Lorcan, the sort of youngflas who'd carry a screwdriver instead of a blade.

When a Wren eats cooked meat, they'll rub the juices on their necks like it's a perfume, to advertise to the laneway that they've been eating like princes. Lorcan's attention is too stuck into the rendering screen of the Slumbo app to hear when they crawl up behind him. But a dark gust carries that scarce fragrance of greasy beef and it slides up Lorcan's nostrils and down to his tongue. He salivates and turns to face the smell. Fuck, it's the two boys.

Scunter: Show us your phone, Lorcan.

Boulevard: Fuck you doing down here, Towerboy?

Scunter: You after doing a Slumbo, is it?

Lorcan: I'm only looking for a bit of reception here, lads. I haven't slept since last night – and I deleted it anyway, wasn't worth the look.

Boulevard: We seen the purple light coming off your wrist from inside the car, Lorcan. We were watching from back there the whole time while you were asleep, like.

Scunter: Why are you lying to us, Lorcan? You asking for slaps? Give us the phone – we only want to see.

Lorcan: It's not rendered.

Scunter: Are you watching this foxy cunt here, Boulevard? Cheeky prick with his filthy petrol exhaust. It's ones like him who killed all the geese stone dead.

Boulevard: Choked them out of the sky. And the wasps too. No geese or wasps because of him and those like him.

Scunter: He's lying to us, after we saw the wrist glowing purple and all. He's cooking up a Slumbo, alright.

Lorcan peeks through a blindy breeze that brings sand with it, trying to size up the severity of the brothers' expressions through the murk. The night wind belts off the Wrens' blocky faces. It doesn't bring on a squint like it does to Lorcan. The Wrens can stare into the wind down here in the lanes.

Lorcan: I wasn't lying. I don't have one now. I will have one – it's just not ready. There's shit reception or something. It won't render to the app.

Boulevard: He's been banging Aoife Tannam from the 2012 Punto five cars down. I seen the two of them last week shifting in the backseat of his Flapmagnet.

Scunter: Are you having dreams about her, you fucking pervert? And then you'll have a greedy wank at it down this lane? What would you be doing if we weren't here? Pulling the belly off yourself, is it?

Boulevard: I'd say you're right, Scunter.

Scunter: You sick bastard, Lorcan. Is that why you won't show us the Slumbo? I bet you got a good look at her – she stuck into your mind, every crease on her, and the passion inside your heart too, the longing for it, boy, loads of detail, the triumph when you came, is it? Is that what's on the Slumbo? Let me feel that triumph. You twisted greasy gowl. You make me sick.

Lorcan: I don't even know her – what would she be doing even talking to me? She doesn't know I exist.

Scunter: My hole. Show us your thoughts of her, or I'll take it off you and give it to Uncle Deccy. He's mad for notions of young wans.

Boulevard: Deccy'll come looking for her if he gets a squint of a Slumbo of her. Show us now, and Deccy Wren can stay out of it.

Lorcan: I don't get dirty ones.

Scunter: What ones do you get, then?

Lorcan: I dunno, stuff goes wrong with the rendering. It doesn't pull down the images off the servers properly – they get mashed up or something – and then the Slumbos come out gammy. I just delete them.

Boulevard: Spoofing fool. He's hiding memory tits in that. Will I take it off him, Scunter?

Scunter: G'wan.

Boulevard lurches forward with a scabbed fist and snatches the phone from Lorcan's hand. The Slumbo has rendered. Scunter lays his shoulders behind Boulevard and his inch-thick rose-gold link chain is dwarfed by the big mad neck on him. The phone screen makes the laneway glow. A rush of anger throbs into

Lorcan. He has a think about taking the phone back until he sees the healed-over cuts and burns lit up on the Wren brothers' faces. Dangerous fuckers. Instead, he meekly moves over close to them to squint at the screen.

Scunter Wren pokes a blistery tongue out over his lip, his eyes mad wide with a dog's hunger. Lorcan watches on with a fear over him, unsure of what the Wrens will see. The Slumbo begins to play on the screen in Boulevard's hand.

It depicts a cold bare room. It is a monotone unhappy grey. The floor and walls are one, no brickwork or tiles. Sparse detail. There are no windows, no doors. No evidence of an entry or exit point. The video is mostly low resolution, with flickering moments of high definition. In the centre of the room is a metal bath, filled with water, which switches from being transparent liquid to mercurially opaque at random intervals. A naked elderly man suddenly appears in the bath. He is thin, pale and freckled with liver spots. He has no genitals or nipples. His eyes sometimes disappear and reappear. He raises one leg and begins to wash his calf with a sponge in a back-and-forth motion. At exactly 00:17 of the video the calf is a shaven feminine calf, but it quickly returns to being an elderly man's calf. When this happens, the old man's left leg grows outwards and inwards in rhythm with the back-and-forth sponge motion. The leg then continues to grow outwards only, until it is several metres long. There is no sound in this Slumbo, except at 00:22, when the man's leg extends fully, insect like, to beyond the limits of the room. At this point he utters, 'That's too much. I'm not paying money like that for a train to Portlaoise.' The video ends abruptly.

Boulevard: What the fuck was that? What sensation was that supposed to be?

Lorcan: I dunno, they're like that sometimes.

Scunter: Where were the memory tits? I was expecting a soul horn. I got a bad buzz off that, cuz. I felt nothing from it. Taste of metal and farts inside in my heart after that.

Lorcan: I don't get dirty ones.

Boulevard: Howld on, Scunter, whisht. What do you mean, Lorcan? This is what arrives on your Slumbo? A naked old man with no eyes going to Portlaoise?

Lorcan: He wasn't going to Portlaoise – he said he wouldn't pay the money to go to Portlaoise.

Scunter: Why does he want to go to Portlaoise? Are the tits waiting for him above in Portlaoise? That's put a brain on me like a battered cat. I'll be needing a drink later now. Why was his leg going long?

Lorcan: I don't know. I don't know why any of them are like this.

Boulevard: Well, it was your dream, man. Why are you dreaming about an old lad washing his leg? Who wants to see that? Who'd watch that?

Lorcan: No one wants to watch that – that's why I delete them. I don't put them online. I can't do good dreams. I just can't.

Scunter: You couldn't put that online. Burn it.

Boulevard: What were you trying to dream about?

Lorcan: I want to dream like I'm belting around Limerick in a Civic during the 1990s in the evening, what my brother used to tell me about. I was trying to memorise the colour of the sun before I did a zolpidem.

Boulevard: Jaysus, that'd be a good one now. Didn't Deccy have a Subaru back then too? Some days they were, I'd say.

Scunter: Mortified for you, man, you weird bollix. We stuck the Slumbo on the junkie Conlon with the arseways poisoned mind on him, held him down and shot him his brown, and what we saw on the screen after was weird ta fuck, but there were feelings to be felt from it at least.

Boulevard: Truth, bang of impatience off it there was, got me in the belly. I'd tell cunts I couldn't sleep, Lorcan boy. I'd say I was afflicted with mind damage before I'd show anyone a Slumbo like that leaking out of me onto my wrist. Go'way with your lanky dreams. I'd get the head leathered off me if I took that to Deccy.

Scunter and Boulevard Wren claw away down the lane with the same whispery movements they came with. Scunter throws an eye back towards Lorcan. The creases of intrigued confusion around his mouth melt off into a black shadow – it blankets the pair of them. There's an embarrassment over Lorcan. He's jamming the key quareways into the rusted hole of the Flapmagnet door, locking it shut.

The cornflower glow of the phone licks his face out of the dark. His thumb flicks through the Slumbo app, and he deletes his latest effort of the ould lad in the tin bath. His mind is groggy from jolting himself out of the dream, and the zolpidem tablet from earlier still has him tired. But there's no hope of going back dreaming after the incident with the Wrens. Over by the dustbins an orange cat has a kitten in her mouth softly by the back of its neck. She drags it underneath a rusty old 2014 Toyota Corolla that's stuffed to the windows with blankets and women's clothes.

* * *

ABOUT YOUR NEW SLUMBO

Slumbo is about you. It is about you knowing yourself, knowing others. It is about you being the best you can be. Slumbo's deep catharsis pieces your dreams together from elements of images, sounds or videos already online. The collective visual and auditory reservoir of the internet is cut up and re-assembled by our software into an engaging, fully formed end result based on what you were just dreaming. What you experience on the Slumbo app when you wake up is an accurate interpretation of the dream you just had.

All of the historical data of human online behaviour is source material for the Slumbo to extrapolate from. The taste of your sweat, the beat of your heart, the pace of your breath are all analysed through the Slumbo wrist attachment to inform this process. All you have to do is sleep.

A Slumbo is more visceral than a video of the world recorded with a camera. The camera is a mechanical recreation of the eye. It takes in light, then feeds it back out on a screen in two dimensions – a copy of a very shallow and simple interpretation of reality. Slumbo transcends this. The experience of reality is more than pictures and sounds. Anyone who's ever dreamed will know this. Dreams are more than sounds and pictures. Dreams contain emotions, sensations, tastes.

The Slumbo mines the depths of the human unconscious and can depict intense emotions in a way that video cannot. You will feel hope, anger, regret, ecstasy, elation, sadness, hopelessness and even pain. A fully rendered Slumbo is the epic theatre of your emotions for others to experience as if they were dreaming your dream, for you to distribute to those who matter to you. Share your dreams.

* * *

Lorcan is eating fermented spuds from a bowl in his living quarters. His Slumbo wrist attachment is charging by the wall. The LED is orange and is the only source of artificial light in the tiny enclosure. He watches the metallic smoke coming down on Limerick tonight. It shimmers distant above Garryowen like bloody windshields. Lorcan's box-room has enough room to sit, but not enough to lie down, and enough insulation to not be skinned by the wind. He shuffles to the double-glazed slit of a window and squints down at the lane outside. Moonlight creates a white rectangle on his gaunt face. His fingers are in his mouth again. He's breathing the way goats do, loud and wet from the nostrils, and he's biting the skin of his thumb. Worried eyes monitor the Flapmagnet below. From his window, Fintan's Lane has a broken-head look to it – busted up metal bones of fences lining either side with a worn pathway down the centre. The lane produces wallops and whoops when the streetlights go off at midnight, anxious noises out of the residents who live in the old decommissioned petrol cars that rest up on blocks. The cars glow green and purple from all the dreaming going on inside. The lane stinks of hot piss and chemical liquor and dog shit. The Wrens patrol the lane and batter the cars with lengths of steel wire, just for the noise and the fear of it, all the Wren brothers and sisters selling uppers and downers and Chinese sleeping tablets, opiates and boner pills. Bothering people about their dreams, demanding to see their Slumbos, especially the dirty ones, the ones that don't get shared online – the quare ould dreams, the ones with secrets in them. The Wrens collect them and give them to Uncle Deccy for his hard drive full of everyone else's dreams. Deccy the dream farmer who'll auction your deepest ecstasy or pain online to the highest bidder.

There's cracks ringing out to the left of Lorcan's eye. Scunter Wren is climbing up on the bonnet of a rusty Toyota Starlet – it's groaning pure denty. You can hear the wind ballooning the vinyl of his trouser legs, flapping like sails. The two Higgins twins are glowing purple with the REM sleep inside. Scunter's hounding the bonnet with the metal wire, his mad fringe flailing over his head in the moon. Dead-bird head on him. He's howling hoarse. 'Deccy's hungry, lads. Deccy wants to ate yere feelings with no salt – show us his dinner.' Seeing this makes Lorcan shunt away from the window slit. He lets out a breath the size of a lung. The release of relief. He is experiencing a hum of safety, aware of the privilege of living in accommodation above the lane and not being down inside in a decommissioned car with the Wrens quizzing him every time he sleeps.

There's a faded poster on Lorcan's wall of an old green Subaru drifting, plumes of dirty purple polluting smoke trailing off the tyres. The poster makes his thoughts fly back to his older brother and the mad stories he would tell Lorcan as a young child. How Lorcan would stare up, with his eyes wide open, visualising every detail from Eugene's words. He can see his eyebrow piercing and the thick Dax Wax making his hair shine. Lorcan can smell his brother's spicy Paco Rabanne aftershave in the room, can hear his excited voice telling the stories of racing and modding cars and blaring out tunes, doing doughnuts in car parks and waking up half of Limerick down by the docks. The bright apple red of the Flapmagnet, the first Civic in Limerick to have light strips underneath, big sub bass in the back of the boot. Holes drilled into exhausts so they roar like an obscene metal bullfrog. 'The beures watching, the beures dripping from watching cars, boy, feeling the rumbles of the Civic climbing up their calves.' The forgotten stenches of burning petrol and motor oil that would creep up your nose and trigger a little feeling of excitement in your brain. 'The fumes, Lorcan, you'd nearly want to drink the petrol. Best feeling in the world, man. Buzzing.' Eugene's stories were what the Slumbo app would refer to as Lorcan's 'locus of happiness', the early memories of bliss that all humans experience. The stories were Lorcan's first true feelings of happiness and contentment. *'It is these locus-of-happiness moments which produce the most sharable Slumbo content. Dream happy.'*

Lorcan forgets his box-room and the shit-soaked lanes of old petrol cars that stretch out violently on any bit of dry ground left in Limerick city. He's not worried about the Wrens or the Canavans or the Houlihans or who runs where. He's not thinking about when the stories stopped. He's not trying to remember how Eugene disappeared. He's lost in a daydream of safe contentment rooted in childhood pleasure.

He wraps the rubber strap of the Slumbo around his wrist. It glows green. His mind is calmly focused on the feelings of contentment. He carefully removes a zolpidem from his shirt pocket and slumps into the plastic lounger for a deep sleep and the hope of a dream worth putting online.

The pink slit of morning light has him awake at seven. There's no noise coming in from Fintan's Lane because the Wrens are above resting in their rusty Nest. He opens the Slumbo app on his phone to scroll the timeline of other users' dreams.

The viral Slumbo Yank, Santander Nash, has recently uploaded a dream that has received sixty-four million views in twelve hours. Lorcan watches Santander's Slumbo, which takes place in a vivid green pine forest. It has a detailed soundscape of fresh running water and can elicit the memory of pine sap in any person fortunate enough to have experienced that particular smell in their lives. Lorcan empathically senses intense jolts of wholesome inspiration and contemplative freedom, followed by hopefulness, with a final blast of nostalgia. The Slumbo ends. Lorcan then feels the dark emptiness that can follow the experience of watching a particularly skilful Slumbo. This emptiness becomes a jealousy. Santander Nash's Slumbo was sponsored by two separate pharmaceutical companies – sixty-four million views is a lot of revenue. His teeth grind and his brow furrows.

* * *

Slumbo technology allows you to explore another person's feelings as they happen in their replayed dream. Caution and self-care should be exercised in this respect. Emotions experienced through Slumbo are not true emotions. They are the reflection of an emotion. While the user can 'feel' these, in the traditional human sense, they cannot be consolidated to the unconscious mind. Once the Slumbo is finished playing, you will not retain the emotions you felt while watching it. Despite having a linguistic awareness of what they were, you will not be able to empathically recall them like you would your own emotions. This difficultly to retain the emotional experience can be stressful at first, but do not be put off. Simply rewatch each Slumbo as much as you like, and feel the feelings again and again in the present moment via our app. Dream on.

* * *

Lorcan reads the comments flooding in under Santander Nash's Slumbo dream. They are gushing swathes of praise. 'Thank you, Queen'; 'I felt every second of this. Your dreams are so real, this was just like being in a forest.' Others lie and claim that they can still feel the feelings from the dream.

He decides to open his Slumbo from last night, hoping it will portray the nostalgic happiness he felt thinking about Eugene's boy-racer stories. The Slumbo plays. It is mostly pixelated. It depicts the orange cat that Lorcan saw the previous day. Her fur is slick, more like peach baggy skin than fur. At 00:07 Lorcan experiences a strong scent of burning leaves. The cat opens her mouth as if to meow and human teeth fall to the ground from her jaw. One tooth melts in low resolution. The Slumbo ends. The video produces no feelings in Lorcan, no visceral emotive experience. He angrily deletes it and leaves the box-room for Fintan's Lane.

There's purple sunlight from the smog above the Shannon. When the wind sleeps, the smog has the chance to hang thick and stick in your mouth with its metal taste. There's a sweaty aluminium humidity. Fanta O'Connor is sitting on the bonnet of a rusted-out 2018 Opel Astra. The boot is open to air it out from the night's sleeping. He's wearing a very long red Manchester United jersey with no jocks on underneath. Fanta has the face of a person with a Slumbo addiction. Like a good few others on Fintan's Lane, he consistently returns to the app to watch and rewatch other people's Slumbos on a loop. Continually living the feelings on the screen before he forgets them.

What separates Fanta from the rest is that he has had several viral Slumbos over the past three years which were sponsored by Fanta Orange. Fanta O'Connor has the economic mobility to prepare hot food. The hum of warm piss from the concrete is sedated by the scent of breakfast. Fanta is heating up rehydrated chickpea mash with rainwater using an element powered by a solar panel nailed to the Astra's roof. His face has the type of scars where you couldn't put an age on him. Deep laughter lines trail down his cheeks, carved into him from rewatching Slumbos that make him feel joy and elation. Someone else's laughter lines, played out through his skin. The physical impact of years of habitually abusing other people's dreams.

Fanta: A'boy, Lorcan, how's the head? You saw the Santander Nash this morning, you did? Powerful, boy, powerful.

Lorcan: I did, I only saw it there. I don't like her Slumbos – they're overrated.

Fanta: Overrated my absolute hole, Lorcan. I might as well have been there in the forest, like. It was like being five years old again, with the spruce trees blowing and creaking up in the Clare hills. Did you not get the bang of the pine sap off it? I got it on the back of the tongue. I could nearly feel it sticking to my jumper. Powerful. Powerful.

Lorcan: She's using mods. She's using bots to rob other people's dreams, and those bots farm other people's emotions, so what you see with her isn't actually her dream. It's a fake dream passed off as a real one. That's why they're always going viral – it's cheating.

Fanta: You're a jealous begrudging gomey is all you are, Lorcan. Give the woman credit for having a good dream, will you?

Fanta's face bursts open into a furrow of genuine anger that contorts his Slumbo addict laughter lines. Lorcan peels back his commentary.

Lorcan: I'm just repeating what I read online about her. She's a scam artist, Fanta. Getting paid well for it too.

Fanta: Ya, what you read online off a load of begrudging pricks like yourself who never upload their own dreams coz of whatever banjaxed, twisted shit goes on when ye sleep.

Lorcan: You'd swear you're in a position to talk, Fanta. Every single Slumbo I've seen you upload is the same as the next. The same corny, nostalgic shite with the spider crawling up your arm.

Fanta: So fucking what if I dream about a spider? You telling me the people of Limerick don't want to remember spiders, man? That they don't miss the webs and seeing them eat the flies? That Slumbo got nearly 80,000 views too, cuz.

Lorcan: No one gave two fucks about spiders when they were here. Will you go'way and stop romanticising spiders. No one let them climb up their arms like house pets either. And the spiders you dream about are too big. The spiders in Limerick were tiny.

Fanta: Bollocks. We had a spider in our house – we called him Rusty, and he'd climb up on my da's chest in the evenings looking for rubs. I remember it well.

Lorcan: You get spiders confused with dogs, and it shows in your dreams. I'm older than you. They were tiny and everyone hated them.

Fanta: Show us what you dreamt last night, so, if mine are so corny.

Lorcan: No, there's something wrong with my Slumbo. I dreamt about the orange cat who lives over there near the fence, the one with the kitten.

Fanta: Who wants dreams about cats? There's fucking cats everywhere. Why don't you dream about Brent geese? Or the taste of chicken? Or dogs if you're such an expert on them?

Lorcan: Been trying to dream about bateing around the old city in the Flapmagnet like my brother. I've no interest in having dreams about dogs.

Fanta: Boulevard Wren told us all about you, you fucking lunatic, dreaming about a naked ould lad with a soapy arse and a long leg stretching up to Portlaoise. The inside of you is hollow – there's nothing for you to be dreaming about that's worth watching.

The bitter truth of Fanta's words crawl into Lorcan. He arches forth with a cunt of a red face on him and comes down on Fanta's shin with the sharp sole of a boot. Fanta clutches hold of the boiling pot of mashed chickpeas and takes a swing at Lorcan's head. It misses wide and clatters off his elbow. Lorcan's arm is covered in hot chickpea mush and he lets fly a yelp. The residents of Fintan's Lane throw their heads out car windows to get a gape at the commotion.

Fanta: Off out of it, you dirty eejit. Go on away back up to your tower and don't be bothering me – that's my fucking breakfast you're wearing on you.

Lorcan: It's burning my skin!

Fanta: Ya, there's melted sugar in it.

Lorcan: Who puts melted sugar in with chickpeas?

Fanta: Me – now go'way. Do you not think we've enough to be dealing with down here in the lane with Deccy feckin' dream farmer above in his Nest?

* * *

BECOME A SLUMBO PARTNER

Are your dreams engaging? Are your Slumbos receiving a lot of views? Do they merit empathic comments from other users? If so, our advertising partners want to place their content within *your Slumbos. We will pay you advertising revenue, as long as your content adheres to the Slumbo community guidelines.**

*The human unconscious is a deep reservoir for intense and beautiful emotional experiences. It can also contain uncomfortable memories or desires. To dream this way is normal and acceptable. While scary and angry Slumbos can be very engaging, dream content which is violent, explicitly sexual or portrays illegal activity is not permitted on Slumbo servers. It is the user's responsibility to delete such content. Extraction of this content by using third-party software or equipment will result in the user's account being removed. The trade or sale of extracted Slumbos is illegal.

* * *

The commotion has alerted the Wrens. Lorcan squints up the laneway. Scunter and Boulevard snake down from the Metal Nest towards him, purple sun to their backs, cutting shapes, both glaring white, bar-chested and dragging wires. Car doors shut either side of them like aluminium dominos when they walk past. *Clang, clang.* There are clatters. Fanta drags his cooking equipment into the rusty Astra and closes the door. He cocoons himself in a duvet. The Wrens begin to chirp in a way that's directed at Lorcan but is performatively loud enough for the whole of the lane to hear.

Scunter: What you up to down here, Lorcan? You bothering poor ould Fanta?

Boulevard: He makes a few quid from those spider dreams, man. He's fierce generous to us with that few quid too. A man of the community. Tell Lorcan how much you made from the ad revenue on the last Slumbo, Fanta.

There's a vinegar menace about the Wrens today. Boulevard walks with wide steps and open circus-master hands, a man on a stage. Scunter holds himself stiff, both arms crossed together in front of his bollocks, hands clasped so his shoulders puff out. His eyes are consistent, unblinking and fixed on Lorcan.

Boulevard lashes Fanta's Astra with the wire. Fanta responds all muffled from inside the locked car.

Fanta: Sixty-five I made, Boulevard, and not a bean more.

Boulevard: Good lad, Fanta. Stay cosy inside there now for yourself.

Scunter: Tell us this, Lorcan. Why are you taking dinner out of Deccy Wren's mouth?

Lorcan: I don't get you, Scunter. Was that Deccy's chickpeas? I've chickpeas up in the tower – I can bring them down.

Lorcan takes an opportune turn to walk away. The Wrens want to play with him like a mouse.

Scunter: We don't give two shits about chickpeas. What cunt said we've concern for chickpeas?

Boulevard: Howld on now, Lorcan, come back. Did you ever hear about Ma Wren's goat?

Lorcan: No.

Scunter: Do you know about goats?

Lorcan: They were grey fellas, with horns or a hat. Cat's eyes.

Boulevard: You have it now. Ma Wren had a goat when she was a child, and she'd pull milk up from the goat every morning. The sweetest milk going, cuz, white stuff.

Scunter: Fact – until the milk went sideways. No drinking in it then.

Boulevard: Have you any idea what made Ma Wren's milk go sideways, Lorcan?

Lorcan: What's sideways milk?

Boulevard: Sour fucking milk. The goat was stressed – the goat got frightened and stressed. Just like you're frightening poor ould Fanta here.

Fanta: I'm actually not too bad, lads.

Boulevard: Our ma took milk from that goat. Mr Fanta, here, is Deccy's little goat. Deccy needs the dreams here from Fanta the same way our poor ma needed the milk. There's fierce good ad revenue in Fanta's head. We can't have you spooking him, giving him sour dreams. There's legitimate income in wholesome Slumbos like the ones that come out of Mr Fanta.

Scunter: Taxman loves that.

Slapping the wire on the piss concrete, *whoop whoop*, Boulevard pushes his chest out and roars to the ether.

Boulevard: Not like the rest of these fucking sick perverts on Fintan's Lane, ha? No hope of legitimate ad revenue from the rotten shit ye dream up, is there? Forcing poor Deccy Wren above in the Nest to do business with awful characters online. It's only murderers and paedophiles who'll pay for yere depraved dreams. You'll have us all in jail with the things we have to do to find buyers for the scum rolling around inside in yere heads. Fucking degenerates. And we get no thanks from ye. Keeping ye safe from the ould Canavans or the Houlihans who'd burn ye where ye sleep.

Scunter: Degenerates. Perverts. Sick cunts. You make me want to be consumed by hell's rectum. Making a devil's dildo out of me. *Depraaaaaved!*

Boulevard: I've a very serious question for you, Lorcan. Deccy Wren wants to know why you're down here ateing his dinner.

Lorcan: I'm not.

Boulevard: I'm watching you doing it now, son.

Scunter: Lorcan, lad, if you keep spooking Fanta, you know what? He'll be dreaming about long-legged men going to Portlaoise. What will we do then?

Boulevard: Fanta would lose his sponsorship, and there'd be no revenue for us. We couldn't even call him Fanta anymore.

Scunter: That's Deccy's dinner!

Lorcan: I was only getting some air out here, lads. I'm sorry, Fanta. I didn't mean to be upsetting you.

Fanta: I'm not upset.

Lorcan: Tell Deccy there's no fear of me eating his dinner.

Scunter: Who said you could mention Deccy's dinner?

Boulevard: Why are you thinking about Deccy's dinner?

Scunter: You're not to even acknowledge that Deccy's dinner exists.

Boulevard: If Deccy thought you were thinking of his dinner, he'd start crying above in the Nest with the heartbreak.

Scunter: Why do you want to break Deccy Wren's heart?

Fanta sticks a defeated head up from the duvet in the Astra. He desperately wants to de-escalate the two Wrens. He cautiously rolls down the top of the window, just enough to poke his head out.

Fanta: Don't worry about it, Lorcan. It's only chickpeas. I'm grand. Water under the bridge. Boulevard and Scunter, I appreciate yere concern, but I'm happy as Larry. I might even take a sleeping pill for lunch and have an ould dream about a spider. Deccy hasn't a worry in the world. Ye tell him I said that. There'll be plenty ad revenue.

Fanta retreats his head into the car like a tortoise. Lorcan walks backwards towards his housing block, feeling the glass and screws of the lane crunching under his feet, aware that if he were to turn his back on a Wren, there'd be a crack of a metal wire off his spine. As he reaches the plywood fence that separates Fintan's Lane from the housing block, Boulevard lets out a roar.

Boulevard: Lorcan, Lorcan! We never told you what it was that spooked our ma's goat and turned the milk sour all the while back.

Scunter: You'll never guess in a million years, Lorcan.

Boulevard: It was some big eejit going up and down the road in a red Honda Civic. Fierce loud. Have a think about that before you go to bed.

Lorcan feels a twist in his gut and can sense the cold flush of blood draining from his face. His mouth is agape. The walk on him becomes a hurried shuffle towards the door of his tower block. That new Limerick wind has picked up again and is moving the smog away to the Tipperary lakes. It licks at his legs from the front and slows his gait. The journey is a fight and the wind curls around the tower with a cavernous sad droning song. He switches to a backwards walk when the gusts stab the metal smog into his eyes. An intense fear is consuming his chest. He cannot place thoughts or words on the fear. The clunk of his key unlatches the door of the tower. He instinctually places the weight of his chest against it, for fear of the wind catching it and busting his face open. His heart is in his mouth. With hands on the door's edge he creeps behind it and grabs the heavy chain on the inside. Securing the tower door is a daily battle with the gusts that want to rip it off its hinges. He's well used to it. He puts his shoulders into the pull. The door tugs back at the chain the way big dogs used to. The adrenaline doesn't subside his shock. He pulls the door closed and climbs the grey concrete staircase to his little room.

His lanky fingers shuffle through the shoebox under the plastic recliner and he tears out a blue Xanax pill that he fucks down his gob. He chases it with a zolpidem. The Slumbo on his wrist glows green then purple as he collapses back into his chair. Hours pass as a Slumbo video begins to materialise on his phone. It renders and autoplays. Lorcan is too plastered from the pills to wake up.

A glowing magic-hour orange sun flickers vividly from inside the Flapmagnet. Limerick city outside is spinning when the car does doughnuts. The air is fresh and full of moisture, the smell of chlorophyll and floral notes present. You feel nostalgic and ecstatic. The dewy summer air is occasionally scented with the citrus tang of burnt petrol. You feel excited and druggy. You are sitting in the back seat. You see the skin of your big brother Eugene Dooly's shaved head and the single gold sleeper in his left ear. He is laughing loudly, his eyebrow piercing catching silver light. You feel proud and safe. 'Sandstorm' by Darude blasts from the car stereo. You feel the bass from the boot through the sponge seat in tickles in the back of your chest. A Doppler effect is present in the music due to the spinning of the car. You feel dizzy, fun dizzy. Dust rises as you look out the rear window. You see the full swathe of the old Limerick city centre, streets pregnant with happy evening shoppers. The river is where it should be. There are intense, climaxing feelings of elation, joy, power and youth. The car is now travelling very fast and straight. It suddenly brakes and is careered into a long winding skid. Eugene is roaring with triumph. One hand on the steering wheel, the other on the handbrake, he is in full control. At this point, you feel intense sensations of rollercoaster-type stomach butterflies, a pleasurably arousing blend of fear and thrill. You hear the loud cries of a goat. The car does more doughnuts. The goat's cries grow louder. You hear them through each rear window. The car stops suddenly. Eugene looks worried. He turns down the music. A young man in a vest with tattoos of birds up his neck is walking quickly. He approaches the driver's side. 'Deccy,' says Eugene. 'The fuck did I tell you about acting the bollocks outside my house, Eugene? My fucking family home? The neeeeeeeck on you, boy.'

As Eugene reaches down to undo his seatbelt, Deccy very quickly and discreetly plunges a small screwdriver into the right side of Eugene's neck and head eleven times. Deccy leaves. Blood squirts violently on the windshield and dashboard. You can hear the splashes. This feels like you have been punched in the stomach. Your mouth is open. You try hard to scream, but you can't. Your brother's body continues to throttle with burgundy gushes. You know that the spurts are quick and rhythmic because his heart is beating fast. You try to scream again and you still can't. Eugene's body slumps forward and the weight of this turns up the volume on the car stereo. The spurts become slower. 'Skylined' by The Prodigy is playing. It is too loud and hurts your ears. You are still trying to scream but nothing comes out. This continues for six minutes.

In the box-room, a loud rhythmic thudding wakes Lorcan up. He runs down several flights of stairs and pulls back the metal door of his tower. Scunter and Boulevard Wren stand bare-chested under leather waistcoats.

Boulevard: Give us a look at your Slumbo, Lorcan.

Feel a flush of heat. Mini Babybell
Heart Pounding. Kimberly Mikado
Sweating. Washing up liquid.
An inability to stay still
Jerusalem artichokes? Carrots
waves of deep fear to
the point of feeling like Dying
Barrys tea. Lynx Africa.
Very tight Shallow Breathing
(Caramel) Rocky Bars (Yellow ones)

JO LEE

Bent over, Gonzo Donlon has a string of pure frozen dribble that's hovering down between her lips and the few small stones she's arranging on the Mass rock. Dented convections of dawn air threaten a thaw on the spit stick. A sermon hasn't been said on this altar for the best part of three weeks. Herself and Jo Lee Heffernan are searching for the priest Scanlon. Gonzo's arms are splattered with pricky scabs and itches, made worse by the greasy twine that's holding the burlap sack across her back. Her head is a mouse-brown mad wire halo drooped over a gaunt face of green teenage skin, and her heart is in the past and her teeth are a shore full of shattered shells.

Jo Lee whispers out that the cowld will have kept the priest tucked away for the warmth. Gonzo hardly raises the neck at this. Sound enters her earholes as underwater dumb muffle. Her chest drums a thump of fear up into her mind.

A purple hum of cloud skirts off a heather-bearded mountain three fields over by Gormanlough, with no promise of glimmer bursting through its belly, pure pregnant with rain. Jo Lee flakes her eyes up at the fat cloud and feels a jealousy towards its size and girth.

'Watch that big dirty hape up above, Gonzo.'

Gonzo's eyes stay fixed on the stones. She's on her side, with one hand fidgeting them around and she imagines that they're a half-dozen scuttling lumps of turnips on a plate. She's undecided on whether the six pieces of flint should converge in the configuration of a cross or as some class of triangle. The mind on her is gone blood-dumb from hunger. Her activity is interrupted by a violent retch of green sputum, which dribbles down her chin and onto the pebbles. An attempt at a groan is made. This is met with numbness from Jo Lee, who is now scowling at the imposing cloud, mauve as a brain in the sky, trailing down dirty lengths of distant smudge, broken by a mustard smear of sideways sun that doesn't reach the grass below it.

'I saw you sucking down a thistle top twenty minutes back, at the gate of Aldersmith's plantation.'

Gonzo doesn't listen to this. She splays out on the Mass rock, exhausted from the strain that the wring of puke put over her body. Jo Lee is still fixed on the direction of the cloud and the smell of the wind. If it brings a wetting in their direction, all the journey and work is for nowt. Rain brings worms, and activity from birds and foxes and martens.

'That wet won't come over this way, Gonzo. Get up ta fuck and start looking.'

For six hours in November cold, they had followed the edge of the River Boyne in search of the Mass rock. Crawling over the frost-hardened earth. Every grasp at the soil was a horizontal climb up a sheer cliff. Only last Thursday Jo Lee had gotten her mouth on a ladle of sheep's broth from the soup kitchen in Navan town. Gertie Laffan threw whispers about Father Scanlon missing three Sunday services. At Scanlon's Mass he was known to hand out rations of parsnip, which he stole from the landlord Boyd. It's this parsnip bounty that has the two women up at the Mass rock.

Save for a few ill-advised thistles, Gonzo hasn't eaten a patch of food in fourteen days. The soup in the Navan kitchen is unreliable. Once a week the town blackens in a congregation of starving gaunts. Lines the length of fortnights. A pointless endeavour. The soup is a diluted shimmery broth over a scant mystery-meat brawn. Brewed for hours in large batches, its nutritional value is questionable. When the anatomy is famished, normal digestive mechanisms cease to function correctly. The starving can suffer a painful oesophageal fungus that causes any ingested food to be rejected, followed by an acidic verdigris bile brought up from the liver. The sheer effort that a starving bastard endures to digest food is enough to trigger a state of shock to the nervous system and a failure of the heart. Eating carries a risk with it. The dead are left where they die. Others, dazzled by the famish, follow suit knowing that a drink of soup will put them down too.

'Snap out of it, Gonzo, n'mind giving up now, there's a trinket full of priest's parsnips round here that'll keep us going till the spring.'

Gonzo drops her head, dozy from the hunger journey. Jo Lee lets her rest. She has a few days on her. She has the blast of energy left from Thursday's soup in her. Her eyes gander around the tangles of emerald bramble that surround the grey Mass rock her friend is sprawled across. In front of the monolith the ground is scant, and the muddy footfall from previous parsnip sermons spells out death in the clay. Jo Lee's a day or two away from collapsing. Every flex of her limbs has currency. She won't stand to her feet. The effort and exertion of placing the weight of her torso on her legs would consume too much energy. The very act of focussing her attention, the task of asking her mind to search for parsnips amongst thickets of wilderness, is a measured investment.

On hands and knees Jo Lee takes considered wipes with her palms in the grass, sloth-like, pushing apart green blades. Inching forward, using the full splay of her frame to investigate as much ground as possible without expending too much energy, her crawl takes her to a depression underneath a blackthorn bush. Her eyes turn up from her nose to discover the scrunched corpse of Father Scanlon. The priest lies all birdlike, protruding bones under see-through skin, claws curled round a ragged leather satchel. Jo Lee falls forward onto Scanlon's chest and stretches out, making desperate pinches at the bounty. Her heart feels a loneliness and she rolls on her back with the satchel held above her face, and she scratches at the inside pockets. Wooden rosary beads and bag lint fall down onto her neck. Jo Lee rises up on all fours and starts tugging and pulling at the dead priest's rags, frantic grasps, searching for the treasury of parsnips that had initiated her and Gonzo's quest.

A feathered doom affronts her forehead when she lies back beside the corpse of the priest. There is a tart cotton desert inside her gob, and she becomes aware of the barren howl of her location. 'Tis clear to her that the priest had eaten any food he had before he died of the sickness. Low wind rolls a growling drone over on a distant hill, entrancing her into her own weak thoughts. The boost of adrenaline from the promise of food has deflated. The limbs ache with a wavy pulse each time the chest beats. A frost wind cuts the right-hand side of her face. The faith she had in her and Gonzo's survival is gone. She will die here on her back, beside the curled priest.

She thinks back to a year ago, before the crops grew dirty and wrong. She sees her son Donnacha on bended knees with clumps of straw between his tiny hands, turning and wiring them into the shape of a man. Donnacha's back felt hot when she placed her hand on his shoulder. A breathing sun graced them both with a wave of security and happiness. Across the way was Patrick, skinning peas from their pods in a wooden bowl. His jaw smiled but there was a worry on his mouth. She fights the blinky visions of his crippled body and dry hair. Him howling spew into wet mud. The wicker basket in the corner, hiding the sight of young Donnacha's stiffened body from them both. Every attempt to bring back memories of happiness are assaulted by visions of Patrick's skeletal face and wide-open mouth as he crawled over her thighs and out the door of the hut in search of something to eat or drink. Death all around her under the threat of a distant orange sky.

Her memory is interrupted by a splutter from Gonzo, who is still alive on the Mass rock. Jo Lee feels an anger. As if autonomously, Jo Lee's left hand stretches out with an energy that she didn't know she had. She feels around the body of the dead priest and envelops a clasp of shirt fabric, pulling it taut. In her fingers she feels buttons, which she pinches off. The freezing skin of the priest's stomach under her palm. With a force she begins pulling herself towards the corpse, and up onto her knees. She looms over the body, and sees the faded green copper buckle on the priest's baggy trousers. She removes the buckle, which has blunt edges. Holding it between both fists, she plunges it down below the chest of the corpse, into the soft vulnerability under the rib cage. She begins to drag, and belly flesh unfolds before her, revealing scant dashes of yellow fat and purpled casing. She cuts as far as the belly button and stretches the skin back, opening the priest up like curtains. Innards exposed beneath her nose, and she's thinking back to butchering goats every November, and the lie of the land when it comes to offal. Reaching into the priest, moving past the guts, piercing unknown membranes, touching the spine and searching around the back. Exhuming the liver and kidneys. The kidney is offered up towards the lips.

Saliva warms the walls of the mouth for the first time in weeks. She pauses, understanding that something as rich as a kidney could kill a woman in her state. She'll be dead in under a month anyway, she thinks to herself. It's worth the risk. It wobbles brown and purple in her hand, which is gawky from thick black blood. The top of the kidney is placed in her mouth. She begins to suck gently. The taste of iron invigorates her to her core. She moves her teeth down onto the freezing raw morsel. It has a rubbery resistance like a grape. Her mind darts back to memories of full meals, to the experience of satiation; she is remembering the aesthetic joy of eating. The feel in the mouth of a clamber of buttery spuds. The ejaculation of saliva from under the tongue. The heavenly sensation that is a combination of both taste and smell that causes endorphins to shoot off from the brain and arrive in the stomach as an empty, cavernous rumble. She'd forgotten what eating felt like.

As her teeth bite down on the resistant, chewy kidney, she feels orgasmic with the tension, the expectation, chewing down slower – and then the pop. Her mouth fills with a sharp burst of piss and iron. She chews and savours the penny-sized lump of offal, before the agonising swallow down her gullet.

The kidney scrapes and scratches the whole way down. She is aware of the culinary journey this tiny piece of food is embarking on as it makes its way down her disused food shaft. She feels her stomach muscles whimper from disuse as they push the piece of kidney down into a barren gut. It makes the ringing in her ears rise to a hell-crescendo, makes the headache pound harder. She rests in shivering anxiety, waiting for that familiar retch, that kick in the underneath-the-bellybutton that travels all the way beneath your carriage to your arsehole. The kick that pumps it all back up with acidic green bile, and a painful throat, and a nose full of snot, and bulging eyes, and face sweat that bursts out cold and gasps for breath, and a desire to scream it all out, to shout it out.

But it doesn't come. She waits, it doesn't come. Slight sparks of life dart around her skull. Breathing feels easier. Saliva drums around her tongue. She's keeping the kidney down. She feels the hunger again. Not the sickly hunger from weeks of no food. But the familiar hunger from before the earth got sick. From when she had plenty. From when she'd be so full she'd leave the leftover buttermilk in the bowl for the cat. The hunger a woman has for a second spoon from the plate after a hard day's work.

She bites into the kidney again, this time with relish, with purpose and without fear. She chews it down, savouring the iron, the offal, the urine. She feels scant energy, she feels her life coming back, she feels survival. Gaping down at the disembow-elled priest she cannot find any feeling of inhumanity. The agony of injustice fights back the rules of society.

Her pride has had her blinded. There's food all around, on the roads, in the ditches, in the brambles, in the cottages. She's just never seen it as food. Food has no personality, no thoughts or aspirations, it's just meat. She becomes the worms and the earth, the fungus, the bacteria, the crows. She is nature.

After munching both of the priest Scanlon's kidneys, she takes the liver in her fist and crawls out from under the brambles towards Gonzo on the Mass rock. Gonzo lies flat, in a state that can't be referred to as either consciousness or unconsciousness. In the distance, the fat mauve cloud cracks a groan of thunder and Jo Lee's contempt and jealousy for the thick mass of elevated wet is gone. She hears the thunder as a celebration and she identifies with it. She drags herself up beside Gonzo and pushes away the pebbles that her friend has been arranging so neatly. She pulls away a piece of the priest's liver, pinches it in her fingers. It wobbles cheerfully under Gonzo's nostrils. Her eyes open. There's an anxiety in them. For all her deathly condition and her weakened brain and body, in Gonzo's eyes is a concern of morality that's been triggered from far off in the back of her mind: Gonzo knows that this is human flesh.

'Ate it. Fucking ate it, or die on the rock.'

Gonzo is not responsive. Jo Lee wipes the liver piece on Gonzo's lips and in around her yellow teeth. A tongue darts out, and a puff of breath. Jo Lee notices the wretched fish-egg stink from the breath and is enamoured by it, feels a sense of victory that her body is registering smells again. Jo Lee has a determination, driven by fury and tears. She thinks back to her son Donnacha dying from the sickness and hunger in her lap, Patrick pulling his hair in bawls and hysterics in the corner.

Jo Lee offers the liver to Gonzo's lips. Gonzo chews. Jo Lee uses her new strength to wrap her arms around her friend. She gently sits her up, knowing that the fibres in Gonzo's body won't have the strength to pull the liver down and that the assistance of gravity is required. Jo Lee has Gonzo in a hug, her head is resting on her shoulder. Behind Gonzo in the distance is the furious bastard of a cloud roaring out thunder claps and letting out flashes of activity in its fat folds. The cloud is Jo Lee's brain, taking nutrients and vitamins and energy, flashing activity and electrodes, sending power to the muscles.

She can feel the activity in Gonzo, can feel the liver working down her oesophagus and producing a resonant rumble that she experiences empathically in her own chest. The liver is animating Gonzo. They both rest on the Mass rock. The cloud has spread out, gone from black violent purple to that cynical Irish grey. It rains down on top of them. The freezing rain is a welcome sensation on the skin of two women who've just got their energy back. They feel it dance on their bare toes and tickle down their cheeks to their chins. Gonzo sucks rain from her lips to wash down the liver. Her eyes stare at nothing, pupils like a stagnant pond. The flesh taste is carving a future trauma into her mind. They both get to their feet and make work on the rest of the priest Scanlon, eating with fervour each of his lungs. The rain washes out the blood from his body and pools in the open hole of his belly. Jo Lee reaches into the blood water and tugs out the heart, places it in the leather satchel for later. Gonzo watches on, her teeth gritted together, her wild tangle of curls flat and wet against her forehead.

'Have you no respect at all for the man? Would you not leave the heart in his chest?'

'What use or difference is a heart or a liver or a kidney to the dead?'

'We'll both see fucking hell for this day.'

'We're living in hell, Gonzo. This is hell. The only heaven I see here is the maggots' heaven, getting fat off the priest if we'd have left him.'

'You had this planned, didn't you? You'd no intention of coming up here for a bounty of parsnips? You knew he'd be fresh from the cold weather.'

'If I had it planned then I wasn't aware of it. But some force guided me. Brought me around to my senses, while I was dying with humanity, with pride. Fuck that shit. I'm out here surviving. Look at you, standing up straight, with a sparkle in your eye. The second you're around to your senses you're throwing guilt at me.'

Gonzo backs down. Jo Lee stands tall. Her skeletal hands, enveloped like a parcel, tell tales of her past life breaking horses by the lough. Jocking wild fillies, shoving ropes in their mouths, tugging a tameness out of them until their lips bled and her hands burned. Fine money at the market for a tamed horse. Tough fucker is Jo Lee.

She looks down towards the sparkle of the Boyne, a quarter mile away, and both women bend down the hillside, erect with their bellies full of priest. The sky has darkened to a curtain. The road near the river is a carved-out mud path, every dandelion, thistle or tree-bud has been stripped by the starving. They spot a gang of mudlarkers crawling on the silt shore, up to their oxters in stink sludge. The air smells like eggs. It is the Dennehy crew, their numbers diminishing by the week. Paddy Dennehy once made a fine living from mudlarking, crawling through river sludge with his brothers, retrieving bottles, vases or scrap metal from the ships that made it up the Boyne. If they were lucky they'd come across a Bellarmine jug, a ceramic vessel of odd shape, given to navvies for rum rations, with carved-out effigies of mad wild woodmen overgrown with hair, fluttering around forests like animals. The jug thrown overboard by a drunk scut whose sea legs gave him a blast of anxiety when he caught a glimpse of coast for the first time in six months.

'Any joy, Paddy?' calls Jo Lee.

Paddy Dennehy's white eyes look out from a body covered entirely in thick black mud. There is no verbal response out of Paddy, the hunger has him ready to go. Paddy is searching for mussels on the shore, to no avail. The river life in the Boyne has disappeared over the past six months. When a man dies in his cottage, leaving behind a horse or an ass, the starving animal instinctually travels towards water. Hundreds of ownerless horses and asses have gone to the Boyne to die on the shore since the hunger began last year. Their decomposed bodies fill the current with a putrefied effluent, poisoning every perch, eel or mussel for miles downriver and putting the thirst on Navan town.

'Give him the heart, Jo,' says Gonzo. 'Tell him it belongs to a sheep. Look at the state of the poor cunt.'

Jo Lee obliges. She reaches inside the leather satchel and removes the priest's heart. The black mud dangle of Paddy's face cracks a white smile that looks like a half moon on a June night. He carefully places the heart in the crusting pocket of his tunic, in amongst the mud, as though he won't eat the heart in the presence of another for fear of having to share. Paddy then hands a Bellarmine jug to the women.

'We'll take that into Navan and sell it to a sailor who's lost his,' says Gonzo.

'We can't go back into town,' says Jo Lee. 'They'll see the life in us. They'll think we've been robbing food from a landlord.'

'What if we crawl?' says Gonzo.

'I'm not getting back down on my knees. We've to continue what we started.'

Twenty minutes away, down the fields by Gormanlough, is a collection of abandoned cottages. The two women venture down to rest their heads for the night. When they get there the familiar signs of death are present. Disused milk churns, scraps of fabric in the muck that probably had bones underneath. They push open a door to a barren space. The tin roof will keep them dry but the open window lets in the cold.

'I'm feeling the hunger again, Jo Lee. Where will we find something fresh?'

'There's nothing around here, Gonzo, we might have to travel as far as Drogheda. Anyone who was here is long gone, their remains would only make us worse.'

A silence comes upon them, their hopes dashed. The priest was a lucky find. Anyone alive is going to be congregating near the towns in hope of soup. The towns are a hostile place for two beures with a look of satiation on them.

As pitch darkness wipes over the room, a small blast of yellow light becomes apparent in the distance. A cottage above on Neary's hill has a hint of a candle in the window.

The pair leave the abandoned hut and venture up towards the light. As they draw closer they slow down their pace so as not to spook the inhabitants inside. Jo Lee creeps up to the gable window to take a look inside. Sitting around a single candle for warmth is an elderly woman. Not long for the world by the looks of her, but clearly in ownership of some type of food, if she's the only one left.

'I think that's Ita O'Donovan, the cooper's wife,' says Jo Lee.

'Hasn't she sons?' says Gonzo.

From the emptiness of the cottage Jo Lee can tell that Ita has sold every possession she owned, from her husband's tools to the kitchen table and the cooking pot. These are all the signs of a woman whose sons have been given the money to leave the country. She is alone.

Gonzo has the rumble in her tummy. Her previous morality has drifted away and the urge to survive has overcome her.

'What'll we do? Should we wait for the hunger to take her? Lamp her frame, all shivers. She hasn't a hope. We could go back to that hut for a day or two and wait. Then come back up when she's dead. If she can light a candle, we could light a fire in that hearth and roast her.'

'An ould one like that could hold out for a week, Gonzo. Look at the eyes on her. Every wrinkle on her face is a past bitterness. She'd be stubborn, she could last longer than us. You'll have to go in and kill her.'

'I'll have to kill her? Why would I have to do it, Jo?'

'Because I ripped open the priest and saved your gowling life, and you embarrassed me down by the mudlarkers, putting me on the spot like that, forcing me to trade the heart for a fucking ceramic jug. You're the reason we've the hunger darting back on us.'

Gonzo creeps off like a bowld cat towards the door of the hut, while Jo Lee bowzies outside the window. Jo Lee notices a small brass box under the ould one's chair. Gonzo has the adrenal bulging veins of someone who's about to murder. Jo Lee worries that Gonzo's thumping heart might send a rush of blood to her head that would knock her unconscious and alert Ita O'Donovan.

With a gallant foot, Gonzo buckles through the door bolt and has the ould one on the ground in instants. She kneels over the woman's chest and dashes her head against the hearth several times over, overcome with the famish. Ita's limp skull pools blood across the honest slabs and Gonzo bends down to suck it off the ground. Her mouth is tingling from the memory of the priest's liver earlier that day. She's gone greedy.

While Gonzo is contorted on top of the woman, Jo Lee appears behind her. Taking the priest's buckle that she stashed in the satchel with the heart, she pounds it into the back of Gonzo's neck. Juttering and staggering it into the cord of her spine, killing her in seconds, like the way you'd kill a crab.

Now Jo Lee paces back and forth with a loathing dread across her. She reaches for the brass box under Ita's chair. When she opens it up, there are metal coins inside. Either the ould one's sons are still around, or they died before she could give them the money to leave.

Jo Lee takes the buckle to both of the bodies and removes the soft organs. She teases a vulgar kidney over the flame of the wax candle that the ould wan had huddled over for warmth. The forgotten smell of cooked meat floods her nostrils and translates into her mind as hopes and dreams. She feeds herself good. She fills her belly until a sleep folds over her.

Cornflower morning light excuses itself into the cottage that honks of iron from the cooked blood. The candle is extinguished. Jo Lee phoenixes up with a strength in her legs that she hasn't felt in months. With the strength comes a guilt. She refuses to let her eyes hit the floor. A dull sickness maroons her torso, followed by a fear that the guilt will make her puke up the fullness in her tummy. She leaves the cottage with a refusal to look back or think about what has happened. She thinks back to her son Donnacha, with his bowld smile and curious eyes and fidgety hands, Patrick with his fine shoulders and unapologetic laugh that would howl across a valley whenever one of the cats did something gas. His deathly face and sickened posture do not intrude on her memory this time. She has the strength in her to push those thoughts back, to remember them in life and not in death.

She heads south below the Boyne, across the heather dells, through the mud. The sky has cleared from the day before and a blue frost is back. She passes a ragged donkey with a dumb stare and protruding ribs, heading for water to die. Upon reaching the Glencoole bog she comes across the triangular-shaped rock that leads to her old holding. The tiny hut where she lived a happy life comes towards her from the distance. She carefully walks up to the yard of the farm. Nothing lies where it was the day she left. Her horse reins are gone, taken by scavengers, the butter churn gone too. Only the stone hut without a door is as she remembers it.

Vinegar dread climbs up from her chest to her forehead and tingles down to the end of her limbs. Her breaths are large and laboured with the terror of seeing the remains of her son and husband. There they are, as she left them. Patrick's rags are pressed against the floor, his skeletal bones and the brown skin taught across them like a bodhrán. His mouth wide open. She carefully pushes over the wicker basket to see the collection of bones and fabric that had been her little son. The body she and Patrick refused to acknowledge, such was the distraction of their sickness.

Going out to the bog and the side of the gable, she gathers armfuls of dry heather from under logs and places them in the hearth of the fire. On the mantelpiece she finds the naps of flint she had used to light many a fire to keep her family warm. With purpose she cracks them together and bright sparks flicker onto the dried matter. A flame engulfs the fireplace. She carefully collects the remains of her son and husband, and burns them down to dust. The funerary respect she affords the remains bring about an internal queasiness. She wonders why these remains are people but the priest, Gonzo and Ita O'Donovan were just food. She wonders if she can ever live among other people again.

When the fire has burnt out, she takes the Bellarmine jug that Paddy Dennehy's mudlarkers traded her for the heart. She wipes it clean. It is a tan ceramic with a custard gloss. Its raised edges depict a bearded man with hair all over his body, a mad savage of the woods. With a careful hand she flows her family's ashes from her palm into the jug. Jo Lee screws it closed. She pats the ould one's money in the satchel. She's taking the ashes on a ship.

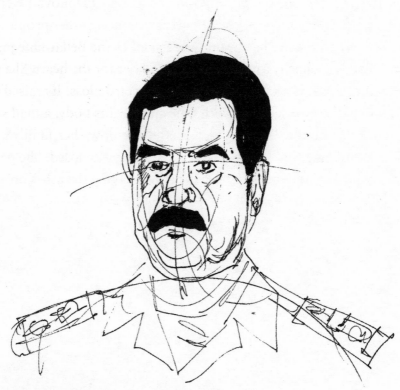

IF you are worried. Shout your problems into this drawing of
Saddam Hussein. And they will go away.

GRUYÈRE IN THE DESMOND

'The Greeks would want a word with themselves now with their hard cheeses.' That was the Chin's reaction to the halloumi, having previously tasted the feta. To which he asserted, 'I don't need to be hearing my food squeak inside in my head like a rat.'

The Desmond Arms was a grand pub. Nothing fancy – not manky either, though. It was grand. Bang of lemon cleaner off the jacks floor but a desperate withered hole on you from the worn seats. It would normally be a quiet pub, too, until we'd take out the cheese in front of the Chin on Tuesdays. Guppy would travel from Tesco with a selection, and there would be a blindfold for the Chin, made out of a tea-towel. And then Guppy would impale the little piece of cheese on a cocktail stick and hover it in front of the Chin's open mouth, and you'd see little flickers of terror in his body, jiggling the fat belly, jolts, fear of the surprise of something new. The whole pub beyond our group, even the real ould lads, would have their heads in their pints, but in the way that they'd have one ear towards the Chin. Waiting, like it's a penalty shoot-out, to hear the reactions out of him. He'd take the cheese on the tongue and surrender it in, crumbs around the lips and all. And you'd watch his face dragging and pulling. Head on him like a terrier with a ball. A groan would be let out. I don't think there was ever a cheese he liked. And when the groan surfaced, we'd all howl – the whole place would scream laughing. Bellies all over the place.

Guppy would say, 'Out of ten, Chin, what is she out of ten?' and the Chin would say, 'She's a four. What did you call her again?' 'Gruyère,' Guppy would say. The Chin would purse the lips again, and you'd know the pokey tongue was searching around the gob to assess the situation. 'She's like a Kerryman's dustbin.' And the fucking pub would shake from men's laughter. Guppy would go up to the dartboard and write on the slate: 'Gruyère 4/10, Kerryman's dustbin'. The blindfold would come off the Chin, and he'd be clean into a Carr's cracker and his IPA to wash down the cheese.

Gruyère was the last cheese the Chin tasted before they found him hanging against the door of his upstairs bedroom. He had taped off the bottom of the stairs with a full roll and stuck a little cardboard sign on the tape barrier that said, 'Dont come up the stares, just fone the guards. I am sorry', so as his daughter Ciara wouldn't have to see his body.

Stilton, Gouda, provolone, Munster, Cheddar, pecorino, Camembert, mozzarella, Havarti, ricotta, Edam, Manchego, Roquefort, Emmental. You might as well have been carving those names into gravestones up in Mount Saint Kenneth.

We started the group in 2015. There were sixteen of us. By 2019, that was down to eleven. Jarlath Purcell, 53; Ger 'Rusty'

Riordan, 48; Caleb 'Elbows' Wallis, 52; Finbar Kinsella, 49; and Bernard 'the Chin' Collopy, 50. All dead men.

The Brothers of Gatch was a weekly meet-up of some old pals from school. A gatch is a way of walking, a stride on you, like an 'I'm-not-here-to-start-hassle-but-I'll-finish-it' kind of a gatch. The group began with myself and Guppy in the Desmond Arms, 24 March 2015, for two reasons.

The first reason was the situation with the taps. The Desmond, I knew, for thirty-odd years, had only ever four taps: Guinness, Harp, Budweiser and Bulmers.

But then they brought in the craft beers to draw a few students – at first in bottles and then on tap. The students never came. But men get curious. And you'd have a Saltwater IPA or a Saison or an Oyster Stout – studied sips, then hungry gulps, before realising you'd been missing out all along. And four taps turned to twelve, and two taps would have a guest beer each month.

The second reason we started the Brothers of Gatch was the new selection of cheeses below in Lidl and Tesco. Mad quare beige lumps with names that sounded like they fell off buses. One night, myself and Guppy were drinking a pair of sour grapefruit ales, and he said, 'Sure, this is like wine. We might as well have cheese too.' So we did. I strolled over beyond to the Tesco across on Mallow Street and plucked a few odd cheeses out of the fridge. Brought them in the door of the Desmond, placed them on beer mats and we ate them with fingers on us. Started ordering different beers out of the taps too, and tasting them with new cheeses, mix-and-match, like, and it was powerful. It brought something to the pub, to myself and Guppy's friendship. I don't know what it was, but it wasn't just pints anymore. It wasn't dark.

When the cheese and the craft beers were brought in, it felt like a game, and you'd be excited for it every Tuesday evening. So we invited more men in, fine men – clerks, joiners, engineers, men we knew a long time – and we'd all have a new craft beer and a new cheese each week, and we'd talk about it, hop ball, write reviews on the dartboard, and it was like being back in sixth year of St Clement's again.

There was a third reason we started the group. We never spoke about the third reason. Even though the third reason is more powerful than the first and second reasons.

There's a blackness that comes over men. It's a dark fright. And you can't look straight at it, and you can't say out loud that it's there. But you know it when you feel it first thing in the morning and you just can't figure out what the point of being alive is. The thought of that brings this sharp dread and after that, I suppose, an olive sadness – no, a green loneliness, a feeling of being trapped purely by just being awake or alive. And it will slowly take away all the things you'd normally enjoy, like a film, or a match, or a song. And it will slice bits off of you until you need a pint to clean the wound. And the pints won't even sort it, they only numb it. That was the third reason we started the Brothers of Gatch. In from the hovering grey cold of Tuesday nights.

The third reason would only be noted over Emmental or a cloudy cider, through purple skin under eyes and red noses. Little yellow glances at each other. Never words. Just gestures. Through slags and pats on backs and digs in shoulders. I knew. He knew. They knew. This was never about cheese or craft beer. It was an unspoken contract. Turning our faces away from the forever pull of the solitude. It was an agreement. We all suffered under the same loneliness. Not the loneliness of being alone, it wasn't that – sure, we all had our families and wives – but the mystery emptiness of feeling alone when you're anything but.

On nights with pints I'd stare up at a bottle of Cutty Sark above the bar – the yellow and black label with the ship would draw me in. It had about twenty sails, and I'd think of myself at the helm, and all around are little islands, and I'm searching them for the man I used to be. He's lost, but in the heart of me, I know he's gone. And I sail on the big mad nothing sea that screams wind in my face. I investigate from island to island. I find fuck all. I still wander into the dead bony forests and shale rocks. And one day, I'll go so deep into one of the islands that I can't see back to the ship. On that day, I'll lie down against a tree and let death have me. That's a cunt of a way to be.

And if I'd ever get that look on me, staring up at the Cutty Sark, one of the lads would draw me back and ask me what I thought of the Stilton. They were like a lighthouse. Just something glimmering off in the distance for me to reach towards. Something different than the empty islands.

Lüneberg, Nut Brown, Herve, Red Ale, Danish Blue, Weiss, Clonakilty Swiss, Blond. In the map in my head, the islands became a cheese or a beer with each expedition.

We began to notice our own little dark rituals – the moment that your head would leave the pub and you'd entertain the dread. The thousand-yard stare, I suppose, but we'd never been to war. For me it was the bottle of Cutty Sark. After Caleb Wallis was found below in the river, God rest him, Guppy went back on the John Player. If he went outside and took too long, you'd see him standing and gazing, the fag long with ash down to the butt. Him drifting in towards the empty. I'd want to ask him what he saw when he stared, but you could never ask that. And you'd shout, 'Come in before Jarlath eats all the Roquefort, you fat prick. What's keeping you?' And he'd say, 'I was going to come in five minutes ago, but your mother offered me a soapy diddy wank behind that red Corsa for a fiver. Big long leathery nipples on her like monkeys' fingers.' And you'd roar, 'Ya, coz you've the massive bar of soap hidden up your hole like a cock, you bender.' And we'd laugh and he'd come back into the pub, and then you'd have saved him.

For John Paul Noonan it was when he'd start picking at the label off his beer, so you'd get him a pint glass. Eddie would take his jacket on and off like he was leaving. Finucane might go to the jacks for a very long piss. Christy Walsh would touch his chest and ask what the symptoms of a heart attack were. Andy Fitz would get a blank stare and snap himself out by starting an argument with you. The Chin, the poor ould Chin, would have pink eyes with tears over them, and that's when we'd give him a blindfold and give him laughter. These were little devices, unique to each of us, that would let the others know that you were staring at the emptiness. And we'd all know this, but we'd never say it, and we'd save each other every Tuesday night.

'Go for a run,' my doctor would say to me. 'Have you tried meditating?' 'This happens to men of your age. I'll book you in for a prostate check.'

The Brothers of Gatch knew what was wrong without words or diagnoses. When the Chin was fifteen, he was smaller than us, and we were in Inter Cert year. Our schoolbags would be three stone with the books. Tough slog, but you'd stick with it. One evening in April, as we moved up through town after school, the Chin stopped and couldn't go on any more, blue asthma inhaler up towards the teeth and a hum of onion sweat on him. His bag was too heavy. He slanted against a wall to rest and asked us to stall. We called him a fat smelly queer and walked on.

This is just another Tuesday in the Desmond Arms, and what's left of us are in the black suits. There's no craft beer or cheese when the suits are on. Just porter and silence. Guppy is outside in the sour rain, his fag long with the ash. I think about mentioning the third reason, saying it out loud, saying it to the group. Putting a name to why we're all here on the day of the funeral. I don't. I look up at the Cutty Sark, and I see the Chin walking off to his island.

WIND MILKER

My da never told me anything about my mother or why she went away. And to be honest, it's not something I'm too fond of thinking about or even asking questions about. Sometimes I do think about it, and when I do, I imagine the reason she left was because my da was a lying cunt, and then I don't feel annoyed or, God forbid, abandoned. I say fair play to her. I look into the mirror and I say, 'Fair play, Ma.'

There was a period of about fifteen years in Tramore, from around the mid-seventies up as far as Italia '90, and during this period, if you bought a carton of milk in East Waterford, chances are it was from one of my da's cows. There was the Quinns' farm – they had a medium-sized herd and would make deliveries to the creamery – but mostly, the milk in Waterford came from our farm. Cussens' milk. And you'd taste it. There's a flavour to milk that's from a herd pastured in a sea breeze. Umami, the Japanese call it. Seaweed has it in droves. You wouldn't know it, but the milk we produced had an oceanic umami when it hit the middle part of your tongue. I said this to the lads in school when I was twelve and Kevin Hennessy, whose uncle was a priest, overheard and called me a spoofer. When I told him to fuck off he threw a metal pencil case at me and it left a big cut above my eye. And then Da told me I didn't have to go to school anymore. So I stayed at home, and I got good at ferrets, and I learnt how to herd the cattle and drive them to the creamery. And Da would play the music of John McCormack for the herd, on the stereo of his Datsun, because McCormack was a big fucker from Athlone with hands like squash rackets. And Da would say he wanted the milk to have the taste of the sea and the taste of what John McCormack singing sounded like.

My father was a liar. He'd lie about his supper. He'd be eating a slice of toast and he'd tell me it was rice. When I'd say that rice is loads of smaller bits in a bowl, he'd tell me that it was a new type of rice that's very big and I'd never seen it yet. He had a pair of big woolly slippers that he'd wear instead of buying carpets, and he'd tell me that they weren't slippers but that he had a rare genetic condition that caused his feet to look like slippers and that I might inherit it. And so I'd shave my feet, even if there was no hair. I'd take a razor to my feet and shave them clean. Sometimes I still shave my feet. He wasn't a bad man. The greatest lie my father ever told me was that he'd leave me the farm. I'd lie back in bed at night with shorn feet and think of the cows. Think of myself, on my own, no Da, and my ferrets down my cardigan. And I'd think of driving cattle with a big stick. And I wouldn't be playing John McCormack – I'd play them Bryan Adams. Whenever I'd imagine this, I never saw myself as an adult man, but rather a type of very long child, because I was only nine at the time.

This is how I came to inherit Sycamore View. Not inherit in the good sense, in the way that I'd have a few euros under me, but I inherited it the way you'd inherit woolly-slipper feet or a lung complaint.

Sycamore View is a retirement community. It is owned by a private equity fund called Bridgewater Capital. It's a bloody expensive retirement community of sixteen 'chalets', full of ex-civil servants and bankers and headmasters who never had any children. They come here to live in a pre-death fabricated purgatory when they can't be trusted to deal with the dementia or the corduroys. They sell their house to the fund, and the fund puts them up here for that last few years they have left. A 'fair deal' agreement is what a solicitor would call it. The few acreage of farmland, where my birth-right umami-milk cows once cudded, is now a bastarding retirement village, with my original farmhouse bungalow still at the entrance. Except it's not a farmhouse anymore – it's the 'reception area', and I'm the receptionist and the caretaker and the herder of codgers.

Bridgewater, the Canadian venture-capital cunts, swindled my da into leaving them the land in exchange for seventy grand in Judas's silver before he died, on the contracted condition that I be provided with employment. And he didn't do this out of love or care for myself, not a chance. It was an act of competition. He feared that I'd produce better milk than him after he died. 'Oh, Jaysus, you'd miss the milk from Mick Cussen's dairy, wouldn't you? It had a taste of the Tramore shoreline off it. You'd need to have tasted it yourself, now – I couldn't possibly describe it to you. He was a secretive man, he'd a way of treating the cows and he kept it to himself. Remember when the Asian TV crew came over to film him in '82?' That's all you'd hear down the town. My da didn't want me getting the chance to better him, to take our methodology to the next level with Bryan Adams.

Cussens' milk died with him, and I got stuck working for Bridgewater with the codgers. Of course, the one advantage, the thing that keeps me from swinging myself off a rafter, is that the Bridgewater pricks can't get rid of me. They've to keep me on in the 'reception' until I end up in a chalet myself, eating porridge and tending hydrangeas with a weak liver. It's in the contract. I'm a permanent fixture that can't be uprooted or budged. I'm like an eccentric billionaire's cat who was left the fortune but hasn't the ability or agency to enjoy it. I just lick my balls and eat my mackerel while vultures wait for my death. It might sound like my father was being kind, compassionate, making sure that I'd never be in want of employment. My arse. My situation is a posthumous attempt to stifle me. He wanted the milk to stop with him, but I'll have my milk yet.

The unfairness of this situation is how I found myself nailing a dog's head to my back wall and leaving it there until her owner confronted me. Lavender belonged to Peter Killeen, and by the time he saw what I'd done with her, the flies had been out for days, ticking all over her eyelids and the young tongue that hung purple from the gob. Peter Killeen was eighty-three years of age and had the look of a toddler on him. The memory of a cry. The sun was that orange-juice slant, and it made the small hairs on his head glow from behind, and when that happened I couldn't read his face. So I watched his left hand, and it trembled. He took out a calculator from his chino pocket. He put it up to his ear like it was a phone that he'd use to call for help. He had men's tits through the crocodile of his Lacoste polo shirt.

'Is that Lavender?' he said.

''Tis, Peter. Is that a calculator?'

'Tell me this, Fergus. Where did you find her?'

It was nothing personal against Killeen, or even Lavender. I'd taken her a few days back when she went at my ferrets in the hutch – they can't say no to a ferret. There's a curiosity to sheepdogs that you wouldn't find in a Labrador or a spaniel, and a powerful trust in them too, in fairness.

Killeen stepped a bit to the left now, out of the sun, into the shade beside the cement blocks. I could read all his emotions in that angle. The skin under both his eyes hung a bit, pupils like pools. This meant agony and loss. But then his lips, I could see that they were folded in on each other, citrusy, but not so much that you'd see his teeth, which I could tell by the jaw and temple were clenching down very hard. This meant anger, but not anger at Lavender – anger at me for being responsible for loss and agony. I'd a fierce amount of time for this type of display. That complex interplay of opposing feelings. He was ready. I knew he wouldn't do anything physical. Not like inaction out of fear – sure, he played county in his time – I knew because I could see that his pupils weren't fully looking at either me or Lavender's head up on the wall. They were looking at themselves, into themselves. He was probably trying to remember back through the years, the way old people do, thinking of similar situations he'd been in where someone was directly challenging him, thinking about what he'd do. But he did nothing. The anger and the loss were cancelling themselves out. His muscles couldn't remember how to stop me. He was too old. The memory was too distant.

I'd never done this with a dog's head before. I learnt it from fishermen. You'd use a ham bone normally but I had to use

Lavender's head in this instance. My theory was that if the object (Lavender) had emotional resonance with the subject (Killeen), then the instrument could trigger the necessary responses in the subject. You take a lump of uncooked meat that's on the bone – in this case, Lavender's head – and you hang it up high. I'd chosen to nail her head to the gable wall of my bungalow, more for the theatre and ritual of it than the practicality. But for this instrument, presentation is important. It needs to be almost artistically curated in a way. Flies will go apeshit for bone meat that's up high and in the sun, away from the birds. So they come, and they tell all the other flies, and before long the sheepdog's head is covered in buzzing boys.

This instrument was fairly simple in its construction. The head was about nine feet above us, nailed to the second-last block at the top of the wall. I had twine tied to one of her front teeth, with a pebble on the end, like a plumb line. This was about seven foot in length and hung down into an empty plastic bucket, a clean white bucket.

Killeen was still holding the calculator in his left hand. I don't think he thought it was a phone anymore. He was rubbing his index finger around the rubber buttons, feeling their edges, and then he'd look up at his dog's cranium with a kind of forlorn apprehension on him, and I think he wanted me to explain why there was twine hanging from her mouth. Her decapitated head, that was one thing. He could at least explain that to a policeman on his calculator, but not the twine, or the bucket, or how all three were linked.

The expression he had, it gave me a lot of authority. It was a class of paternal authority that he was handing me, like if I told him why, then somehow all this would be OK and he'd know what to feel. But I wanted to wait. I let him see how calm I was. I was breathing in through my nose, noticing the warm air pass up into my nostrils like a healing light, and I'd feel it streaming down into my lungs. When you breathe like this, after a while you get a sedate little smile on your face, a real neutral face, like a sacred statue. I let Killeen see this on me. Patsy Lavery from chalet number ten came over briefly, but when she saw Lavender, she left, and I could hear how quick her heels were on the road and this meant she was concerned or anxious.

I had planned for Killeen to see the instrument this evening, and I wanted him to play it, and I wanted it to play him. It was five days after I had erected it. I had told him that I'd found Lavender, and that's why he was here with me, with his confused face and his quare pained eyes.

'Look at her,' I said.

Killeen venerated up at the dog's face, high above him, consecrate in stature. The peach twilight battered off Lavender's head and she glowed. The maggots had been eating at the flesh under her skin, so it wriggled, making her jaws move. She was a blood puppet. But the maggots were hungry for more. There wasn't enough on just the head, they wanted the body, but there was no body, so they tried to leave the skull. The instrument was tuning up. We stared silently as the maggots wriggled their way through the dog's nose to the plumb-line twine. They each slowly crawled down it into the bucket below, until it filled with a population of rotund white boys. Three thrushes chirped in their nest over on an oak branch, winding down for the evening. I invited Killeen to get a good gape into the pail, making sure I didn't take too strong a look myself. A swarming mass of maggots in a bucket has a rhythm to it, a strange ould sway. Not a 4/4, closer to a merengue or a bossa nova – you see it first, then you hear it talking to you. Hypnotising. I'd been told before by the fishermen never to stare too long into the bucket. That there were lads who'd have too long a gander and climb up trees and refuse to come down. Or others who'd leave their wives and move to Portugal. Fine big men, experienced anglers, who'd end up in the forecourts of petrol stations in a heap, calling for a manager because they thought the CCTV was making their haircuts magnetic.

'Do you like my instrument, Peter?'

'That's my ould dog's head nailed to your wall with a bucket under her, Fergus. I see no instrument. Do you think I like that, do you?'

This was, unfortunately, a very reductive answer. I also should not have asked a direct question, as it had rattled a slight sense of purpose into him. That's not what I wanted for this perfor-mance. Killeen's face still had that pursed bitterness around the lips and the hurt in his grey eyes. Hundreds of new maggots smell like fresh cum. I don't know if their odour has any influence over the effect they have on the human brain, but it's something I had to name. I suppose it felt right in the moment.

'Don't they smell a bit like cum, Peter?'

I kind of cringed a bit after I'd said that. I knew after I'd heard the words out loud, vibrating from my mouth, that this was one of the things I shouldn't really be saying in company. But there was no response from Killeen, no bit of shock or discomfort or judgement. This was good. His face didn't have the big cacophony of emotions anymore. The small muscles that caused his cheeks and his forehead to move were numbed, and his pupils were big saucers. The instrument was playing him. He stared sharp into the bucket of moving maggots. They rumbled around, little continental quilts. Pulsing. Crawling over and under each other. It was chaos and pattern all at once. Beautiful head music. Peter Killeen's mouth started to hiss and spit a bit – nothing intense, the type of hiss you'd get out of a kettle on a bad hob.

'Could you try making the noise of a bullock please, Peter?' I said.

His eyes were very glossy and distant. He uttered a little moo, like the way a human would moo.

'Not like that now, Peter,' I said. 'Make the noise a bullock would make when they're separated from their herd.'

He let out a 'Mooooooora'. This was good. So I asked him to go down on all fours, and he did that too, and I slid his trousers off, and I reached down and tucked his two long geriatric balls in between his thighs. They felt like warm plums, and he kept them between his legs like he'd been gelded.

'Mooo, rooooooa, mrooooooooa.'

I could see Patsy Lavery watching him from down the road. She looked very serious. I waved at her because I felt happy and powerful. The instrument had shown itself to be effective.

A few days after the ritual with Lavender's head, I was watching Peter Killeen and his wife through the letterbox of his chalet. Himself and Maura had just finished their supper and were retiring in front of the television with a pot of tea and a tray of Madeira cake. I had newspapers under my knees on the concrete step outside their hall door. My intention was to spy on Killeen, to keep him under close observation, to measure how he'd been influenced by the instrument. Sycamore View had a silence over it. One of them foreign nights, with the grand perfume balm of gorse standing on a wind. I like watching in the letterboxes.

It looked like Killeen was experiencing uncomfortable indigestion. His fist rested against the veiny mouth of puffing cheeks, and he mumbled between burps and requested of Maura that she remind him in future to 'exercise caution around plates of onions and the manoeuvring of gammon'.

There was the blue flicker of the plasma flat screen blanketing them as they dutifully watched Radio Telifís Éireann. Maura perched arse first on her seat edge, an electric spine on her, elastic arms that would snap up, rattly eyeballs with an appetite in them, a very alert woman. Killeen, however, was bread-like, stodgy, chewing with a sway to his jaw, ruminant. Looking thick with his jowls disappearing and reappearing under black and blue flickering waves from the television. Below his chin hung a bell, tied with a ribbon. This was not my doing. He had chosen to tie a bell around his neck since our last encounter at my bungalow wall. Seeing him this docile and cattle-like gave me a feeling of hope in my heart.

I'll admit, while I was crouched outside I lapsed in professionalism and began to take an interest in what they were watching on the telly. It was a magazine programme called *Nationwide*, about a bachelor who discovered the relic of an Italian saint in an attic in Cloyne. He spoke through yellow teeth and cradled a three-hundred-year-old mummified human liver as if he were breastfeeding it. This was followed by a segment about fistulated cattle. A hole, or fistula, is cut into the flesh of a live cow and this entrance is then fitted with rubber lips. A perpetual wound is present in the cow's side. It is used as a living window for the dairy farmer to stare directly into the stomach of an animate cow. Herds of cows were filmed from above, and the song 'Yellow' by Coldplay was chosen for the soundtrack. I started to imagine Killeen's house as a big strong cow, and his letterbox that I was looking through was the fistula, and that meant him and Maura were the undigested cud. This made me laugh fierce loudly into the letterbox, and Maura jumped in her seat. Killeen got down on all fours, frozen, his bell rattling. I ran off back towards my bungalow. Behind me, I heard uproarious mooing sounds from behind Killeen's front door, and I was safe in the knowledge that the instrument had been effective.

The Killeen experiment showed me that it wasn't just a theory anymore. There was something to it, alright. A bucket of swirling maggots, if stared at long enough, can create what a hypnotist would call a quick induction. The particular timing of their movements works exponentially – it draws the eye towards the centre, the maggots move in chaos, the brain tries its best to pin down just one maggot, but it can't. There's no pattern to a gathering of maggots, and by fuck we crave a pattern. The brain will burn itself out in search of a pattern. The eyes imagine a little centre and focus in on it, while all the other movement happens around it. Growing intensely with each churn, all reality outside the bucket ceases to exist. Sounds, smells, feelings. It is in this moment of utter trance that a man is open to suggestion: that's the doorway. That's how you get a person to behave like a cow for a few minutes, like at a hypnotist's show. But what interests me is trauma, the shock and awe. Trauma sticks; it hangs on to the brain, tugging at it. The trauma of seeing your sheepdog decapitated, combined with a good maggot induction, will cause the suggestions to root themselves in the trauma. This, if I was correct, would cause Peter Killeen to become a cow or, ideally, a bull at the hint of even the most remote trigger of unease.

In the centre of Sycamore View is a small roundabout, well manicured and fragrant, not like a real roundabout, but a little small fellow, with grass and some shrubs. Killeen had taken to occasionally circling this roundabout on foot. He would drop his shoulder and shift his neck forward in a very guilty way. I was always watching. But when he'd think that no one was looking at all, he'd crouch down with his veiny arms, as if he was about to tie a shoelace, and take a fistful of grass into his pocket like a snake. He then travelled back to his chalet to eat the grass out of his pants with shameful gusto. A good young bull.

At nights I'd take out my mallet, and hammer into the gable end of my bungalow as a siren call, a reminder, to trigger Killeen, to torment him with bangs. And he'd drag himself out from behind his hall door, traipsing on all fours with the bell dingling under his neck. No human vigour in his stare no more, two button eyes that drove a flaccid mind, and then he'd go munch lilacs from their stalks on Bart Murphy's front lawn below in number six, with his forehead risen up because bulls can't see what's beneath their noses. And Maura would be out, shepherding her husband back into the house, wearing her sweaty blue nightgown. And Killeen would refuse and stamp his feet, knocking her over with steamy snorts pulsing out of his nostrils and jowls, his long grey man-testicles dangling, jiggling, catching the amber streetlight. Maura would cry. I'd say, Good bull, Killeen, to myself in my head. And Patsy Lavery would see it all from her curtain, and I'd see her seeing, but she wouldn't see me see, and she'd look very serious.

Dear Mr Cussen,

We received a very alarming complaint regarding an incident concerning the health and welfare of a Sycamore View resident. We are writing to you to remind you of your contractual responsibility for the mental and physical care of the residents. Any disturbance is to be immediately reported to one of the approved on our list of local health practitioners, and also flagged with Bridgewater. This is both for the safety of the residents and in the interest of Bridgewater. It is utterly unacceptable for a disturbance to go unreported.

Yours sincerely,

Paul Mercer

Bridgewater Capital

I watched my bent-over torso in the floor-length mirror, slowly rubbing this letter between my arse cheeks through my Wrangler denims, and then I laughed at myself for being gas. 'Local health practitioners', 'alarming complaint', 'residents' – as if Bridgewater gave two fucks about any of my codgers. Bridgewater had them fully dehumanised. They were inconvenient ink blots in a spreadsheet in a bigger spreadsheet containing all the retirement communities that they owned. Not just here in Waterford – in Ireland, the world. They were doing this everywhere. They only gave a fuck about the houses that my codgers left them to pay for their stay and their 'care'. Flip the houses, make a profit, move on, avoid lawsuits. The ould vultures.

I wasn't going to even dignify this letter with a response because it had an arrogance to it. Who were they to be judging me? They, and I shouldn't even say 'they', 'it' is just a giant pile of cash with some itchy-hole prick getting a salary to write me letters like this. The same Bridgewater owns cobalt mines in the Congo, profits off weapon sales to the Saudis, buys up bad mortgages and evicts the tenants. The same Bridgewater who'd rob me of my dairy farm? Fuck them.

Now that I had my bull, I'd need my herd. This land hadn't had a good strong herd of cattle on it since my da. The instrument was an experiment as such. A dog's head and a bucket. A low-fidelity inexpensive affair. On nights that Killeen would leave his house and go on a violent wander, I would notice a palpable unease over the neighbourhood in the days following. The codgers would go quiet. In July he took a big shit in Nuala Price's driveway while head-butting her side window. It was very loud. Killeen had gotten into a violent rage and had a powerful erection. This really surprised me. Killeen was eighty-three years of age and hadn't had a hard-on in the best part of twenty years, I'd say. But his transition from geriatric to bull had reinvigorated him. This unintended consequence of the instrument was fascinating, and I noted how it might have wider medical implications, beyond the instrument and Sycamore View.

I put this to one side, though, because what intrigued me most was the collective anxiety and pensiveness that Killeen's displays were causing the other residents. While his behaviour was certainly violent and frightening, it wasn't particularly shocking to the elderly community. They read his behaviour as the aggressive onset of dementia or Alzheimer's. Sudden outbursts of violent or exhibitionist behaviour were not an uncommon expression of this complaint. The anxiety my codgers felt was not one of concern for Killeen, however. It was much more of a 'what-if-that-will-be-me?' response. No hint of care or compassion for him. This angered me. Any possible apprehension I felt about my

plans went out the window when I saw how utterly selfish this
was. Killeen's vulgarity was exposing them all to the inner chaotic
animal that lurks beneath our manners, our rules, our nice lawns.
That could be them. Nude, howling, foot-stamping, shitting all
over their long balls. That could be any of them, like time bombs.
Waiting for the brain-shrivel to set in. The mean ould pricks.

At the very least, I knew the codgers by name. I lived with
them. I hadn't reduced them to just numbers on a spreadsheet.
Not like Bridgewater. They just loved saving money, which is
why they immediately put forward the cash when I suggested
how they could reduce the annual electricity bill by 60 per cent.
The Sustainable Energy Authority of Ireland has a grant for
any business which can reduce its carbon footprint by using
renewable energy. It's all part of this global-warming carry-on.

In early August the 7 kW Antaris wind turbine arrived on
the back of a flatbed lorry to Sycamore View, and I signed for
it. Germans delivered it – it was a big deal altogether, a long fat
metal pole with four white foils at the top. I had her mounted
in a concrete base in the back yard of my bungalow, facing east,
just left of the ferrets. She was placed on a small track of ten
metres. This allowed me to move the turbine left or right in
order to catch the best wind. She stood about fifteen metres in
height. There was a piety to her. Big white wings. I began to call
the turbine the crucified metal angel, or just the metal angel, and
I felt that the metal angel was a woman, unlike the instrument,
which I couldn't see a gender in at all. That was more of a thing,
or a contraption. When she got going in a wind there was a
dark hum on her breath. The type of sound that would register
more in your chest than in your ears. *Whoom, whoom, whoom,
whoom, whoom.* Full of bass.

By this stage, Peter Killeen's frenzies had become a nightly occurrence, and he began to live his life less as Killeen the man and more as Killeen the bull. I had manufactured a paddock from old crates on the little roundabout, with a latch. Killeen would spend hours of his day in there. Whenever the codgers would complain to Bridgewater, I would inform Bridgewater that it was under control. Then I would tell the codgers that I'd been in contact with a doctor, and the doctor had told me that there was no hope for Killeen. That he couldn't be healed, only placated. And that this was the wisest approach for us all, to treat him like a good bull, to become part of his new reality, so as not to alarm him. They brought him dry porridge oats, and he ate the oats, and this kept him calm, away from the gardens with his erections and stamping. They would all do this each day, in turns, leaving the hall doors of their little chalets, walking to the roundabout under the watchful sway of the big metal angel humming over them. *Whoom, whoom, whoom.* They were pierced with dread and would not look directly at Killeen as he ravaged his oats and shat. Then they'd walk back, eyes fixed only on their hall doors. He was Lavender's rotting skull.

The humming never stopped – you'd tune it out, but it was always there. *Whoom, whoom.* She would rattle windows in a strong enough gust. A fine lump of a woman who'd catch the same Tramore breeze that carried the seaweed umami in from the coast. I was milking the wind. *Whoom, whoom.* The codgers caught a collective panic. They'd fidget with their hands and develop stomach complaints. They were ready.

Long before I'd had the 7 kW Antaris wind turbine installed, before she was the metal angel, I became interested in the various directions of the sun and their individual effects on my mood.

The way it would introduce itself in the morning, bluish and fresh, sliding sideways and tickling any cold out of the air. In the middays, when the sun was fully erect, hanging off the ceiling like a new lightbulb, hot down on my crown, it would remind me of my bald patch. Sometimes the midday summer sun would fall down on my eyelashes, and my vision would be sparkly. I'd close my eyes to avoid it, or look below, but the white concrete in my driveway would reflect it back up at me. This sun has no colour, this is the sun they crucified Christ in. So I'd just go inside. In the evenings, it says goodbye, the way a friend will beep a horn as they drive off, a reminder to you that they're not gone forever, a comfort. This sun is my favourite sun; it is brown-orange and warm, and even has some violet in it. This is the sun that I nailed up Lavender in. This is the sun that tells the maggots it's OK to come out because the birds are going to bed and have no want for maggots. The sun doesn't pass through the metal angel when she stands still in her track. But if I push her two metres left down her little rail, the sun hits the back of her rotors. *Whoom, whoom.*

When herding cattle, you'd never direct them towards an enclosed space or they'd get spooked, they'd stampede, a situation you'd avoid at all costs. You give them a wide berth, with escape routes and a focal point, such as a water trough. This is why I called the community meeting at the little roundabout. It was 6.50 p.m. in the last week of August. I had delivered a leaflet into every chalet letting them know about the meeting, where each resident would be given an opportunity to speak about Killeen, about his paddock and his behaviour, about our 'options going forward as a group'. He was fully bull. Any drop of Killeen the man had evaporated from him. While he was clearly still physically an adult male human in his eighties, his personality was entirely that of a young bull. I had initially hoped for a gelded bullock – they have a pastoral temperament – but there was obviously a fire in Killeen that saw him become a stubborn full-balled bull. I'd have to work with this regardless. The codgers looked withered, all fidgety knuckles and heads down. This meant fear and obedience. This was good. They gathered in a semicircle around the little roundabout. A gentle chill and a bit of moisture was apparent in the air, the promise of an inclement September to come.

Killeen was in his paddock at the centre of the little round-about. The approach of all the Sycamore View residents around him caused him to snort and adopt a broadside posture. In animal husbandry, a bull who presents the full mass of his body like this is defensive of their personal space. The bull is experiencing a threat and would like to communicate their size and strength to the intruding party. This display places the bull in a physiological state of fight or flight. This was not what I required at this moment. The paddock, however, while not secure enough to contain an actual bull, was more than secure for a man in his eighties who believed himself to be a bull.

Killeen poked his head down behind the blue wooden pallet fence and directed himself at Patsy Lavery. She looked very serious. In a typical aggressive display, he stamped his left hand on the earth and launched his head at the fence. There was a thrilling hollow clatter, which was clearly the sound of human skull against wood. The codgers all puffed up a little terrified *whoop* and backed off a few steps. I bounded over the fence from behind Killeen. I landed quare due to my sixteen stone, but still I mounted his back, with both my feet firm on the earth. I could feel my deck shoes anchoring in muck. His torso was between my thighs, and his head pointed forwards, where my crotch was. I was in full command of Killeen the bull. I grabbed his bottom and upper teeth with both of my hands, separating them, and then I pulled his head firmly back towards my chest, exposing his neck to the codgers. Men's teeth feel very sharp on the fingers when you get a good hold of them. He tried gnashing, but his jaws were no match for the strength of my forearms. The codgers all stared, with new looks on their faces. Mostly terror and shock, but I swear Ernest Naughton had a glint of arousal around the nostrils. I needed them to see me control and dominate the bull. They would not look away. Killeen puffed and roared. Steam flew out his nostrils. The metal angel high behind us went *whoom, whoom*, with the thud of her rotors humming. It was now 7 p.m. The angel was perfectly in place in her tracks for the event. *Whoom, whoom*. The tangerine beam of evening sunlight leaned against the spinning rotors and shone through. Everything now changed.

The chalets of Sycamore View appeared and disappeared beneath a black and orange strobe. The sun was battering my shoulders, and I swear I could feel it get hot and cold with every *whoom, whoom* of the angel's spinning blades. Killeen's teeth were in my fingertips. And in front of me were the codgers. When I pulled Killeen's jaws open, they opened their mouths too as a sort of empathic gesture of fear. And they strobed, flailing their arms in slow motion as the sunlight flickered on them like an outdoor rave. They were all staring at the bull and me. Black, orange, *whoom, whoom*, black, orange. And then it was over. The sun had shifted, and the beam no longer shone through the turbine. Only the sound remained. The codgers had been inducted. The orange sunlight strobe from the metal angel was more entrancing than any swirling maggot.

I said 'Mooooo'. They responded with a loud *mooooo* too and began to drop to their knees. No more complex human faces. Docile, rubbery putty. Ruminant and dumb. They were cows. My hand brushed off my mouth and I tasted Killeen's spit. It had that umami taste that Cussens' milk had.

The excitement had me dismounting Killeen and running back into my bungalow. I needed to be brisk so that they didn't slip out of induction. But I knew in my chest that this was a big one. There was no escaping the trance that a strobe like that would put in you, and with the stress of Killeen in the paddock, I'd say they were nicely traumatised too. My hope was that they had permanently transitioned. I had a cold bottle of blue WKD in the fridge, which I popped open for the occasion. I had my Philips stereo with Bryan Adams on CD – his 1996 offering, *18 til I Die*. I positioned the stereo on the front lawn and let it play, the opening *chang* of the guitar orchestrating this corral.

Patsy Lavery was nude on all fours. She no longer looked serious. Good cow, Patsy. Maura Killeen too. Eamon Callaghan from number eight was devouring sweet-pea flowers from Kieran Fennessy's garden. Good cows, lads. I had my herd and my bull. I circled them all with care, enough distance so they didn't get spooked. I hoped that my lying father was watching jealously from his grave.

And then I let Killeen loose from the paddock. There was a sinful fervour and intent in his eyes, with his giant long balls and red passion, fresh for husbandry. On my bungalow was a security camera pointed at everything he did to them, and in my utility cupboard was a VHS recording it. And when the boardroom of Bridgewater Capital above in Canada sees that tape, they'll be quick to name a price fair lively.

Daniel radcliffe

"I Know Im not a Coal miner. But I do Long hours"

LETTER TO *THE IRISH TIMES*

Dear Sirs,

I write to you in response to your article 'Ireland's Bees in Decline', published in the 22 June 2018 edition of *The Irish Times*, in which my learned colleague Dr Kenneth Burst asserts that the current decline of Ireland's bee population is solely as a result of 'chemically intensive agricultural practices' and a 'decline in biodiversity', producing near endemic instances of what we now refer to as colony collapse disorder (CCD). While such claims are customarily supported by the scientific community as an explanation for global bee population decline, my current research has led me to deduce that the diffuse abscondence of bees is not induced by biological or ecological factors alone. It is a matter of great exigency that the following hypothesis be considered and acted upon by the greater scientific community. This, too, is why I am choosing to write this letter to the national newspaper of record rather than one of the more pertinent scientific journals.

For the benefit of your readers, I will introduce myself. My name is Dr Marie Gaffney, and I am Professor of Ornithology at University College Cork. In 2016 I received the Nobel Prize in Physiology or Medicine. My work focused on the distressing effects of the Cork accent on songbirds. This research culminated in the trial construction of an ecological van powered by the accents of Cork men that was used to eradicate a parasite in the last remaining nesting population of Irish spotted flycatchers, a native bird, once facing extinction, which is now thriving as a result of my interrogations and interventions. As stated, however, this letter will outline my theory on bee decline and is not of an ornithological bent.

Background

In late August 2008, I began as a student biologist in the Krascoe Institute in Geneva, Switzerland, studying under Dr Constance Yop. My research at this point was not ornithological. Instead, it focused on the vibrations of arthritic molluscs when exposed to stringed instruments, a subject that I did not find particularly rewarding. I shared a small lab with the esteemed melittologist, the late Ernest Kinsella, who was then, like myself, a student. The institute had deemed it fitting for us to share, as we were both English speakers from Ireland. Ernest, at this point, was older than me and was a PhD candidate working on an algorithmic interrogation of colony behaviour in European honeybees.

With no disrespect to the departed, I must disclose that sharing a laboratory space with Ernest Kinsella was, unfortunately, a testing experience. Kinsella, in his defence, was a resolute professional, but his passion for melittology was obsessive to the point that it would violate the needs and boundaries of other colleagues, namely mine. It was not at all uncommon for the room to contain several honeybees buzzing about, flying in and out of the window, landing on the desks and, eventually, on our clothes and skin as they became more comfortable in the environment.

Approximately eighteen metres from the laboratory balcony, fixed in a concrete base on the college green, were eight hives operated by Ernest. These were of Langstroth design and constructed from pressure-treated Swiss pine. Eight separate colonies, with roughly one thousand bees each, occupied the hives, and these were the core colonies on which Kinsella's PhD depended. These bees were his children, and he treated them as such, fussing over them with an admirable duty of care and tenderness.

At certain times, Kinsella would be obliged to transport the queen in a matchbox from the hive into the lab for observation. It became evident that the queen's extraction occasioned a distressful tribulation amongst the colony, which manifested as erratic swarming activity centered around my face and hands. On many instances I would conduct my mollusc research while practically covered in bees. They were mostly docile and non-aggressive, and stings were rare initially, provided that both Ernest and I were calm and non-threatening in our physical gestures and emotive expression.

After several stings over the course of months, however, it became difficult for me to conduct my mollusc work effectively in any capacity. The pain would impact my sleep, my levels of stress and thus my quality of research. It became quite chaotic. This would frequently lead to tension and arguments between Ernest and me, including one period of two weeks in particular where we did not speak to each other at all due to a disagreement about his bees. This was quite stressful, as Ernest was one of the only other English speakers I knew at the college.

The bees had an ability to sense tension and conflict and would sting more frequently if Ernest and I engaged in any aggressive behaviours or long periods of silence. They interpreted human tension as a threat. Calmness was essential to avoid attacks. The hypersensitivity of the bees forced us to act in a performatively civil fashion, even though neither of us wished to do so. During the periods that we were on speaking terms, I would voice my complaints to Ernest in joyous tones, with the utmost insincerity, so as not to anger any nearby bees. We both became theatrical actors of sorts, hiding our frustration and contempt from the bees, bottling up any negative emotions, interacting via a type of scripted melodrama. At times, the emotional labour of denying myself my authentic emotions and reactions was more exhausting than the bee stings. I refined a behavioural practice of artificial laughter, in which I engaged during the removal of live barbs from my eyelids. I would also refer to Ernest in very colourful language in a tone that befitted praise rather than the scorn intended. The constituent elements of this uncouth lexicon will not be repeated for your readers. Ernest, in turn, demonstrated a class of nervous tic in response to his contempt for my presence. He would produce a stochastic cacophony of clicks with his tongue.

Suffice it to say, our working relationship became deeply strained. To my shame, when the laboratory environment became too testing for me and I would retreat to the bathroom to apply an antihistamine to my stings, the hand dryer became an emotional crutch. I would scream directly into the hot air.

The noise of the machine would blanket my screams from the potentiality of human detection. This made my eyes very dry, and I developed painful conjunctivitis that interfered with my ability to blink.

On one occasion, I had reason to assume that the bathroom was completely empty. However, Professor Audrey Poise witnessed my bursts of screaming into the hand dryer and reported the behaviour to my lecturers. This did not assist the validity of my complaints about the unconventionality of Ernest's laboratory environment. The incident with the hand dryer had marked me out as being 'emotional' and 'difficult'.

The first collapse

When I complained to the college authorities that Ernest's bees were interfering with my own research, I was largely ignored, told to 'grin and bear it'. After all, I was a lowly undergraduate and Ernest was a PhD candidate. His work was funded; it was 'important'. They were not going to rule in my favour. As a biologist, I was also expected to tolerate stings, bites and all sorts of other 'occupational hazards'. I soldiered on, day in, day out. Bees on my hands, on my food, in my hair. Crawling up the back of my lab coat and nestling on my skin. Any movement from me was interpreted as an attack, which merited a sting. This was my daily life.

This next detail may seem frivolous or anecdotal – I assure you it is anything but. On 12 September 2008, I received some flowers from my dear friend Roy Stunt. To be precise, the flower was *Rhododendron ponticum*. I remember the date specifically because it was the day after my twenty-third birthday, and the flowers were a gift. Roy was a master's student in the botany department. His area of research was invasive plant species.

While he essentially investigated ways to eradicate their spread, he greatly admired their 'parasitic vigour and tenacity', as he would say.

The particular flowers I received had been picked from the wild in Switzerland, personally, by Roy. They stood in distilled water within a ceramic vase. They were very beautiful – immaculate large purple petals with a distinct aroma of vanilla and toffee. These notes provided a welcome change from the more pungent odours of bromine, agar cultures and old wood that permeated the lab. I positioned the flowers in pride of place on my workbench, beside the electron microscope, where they would also receive ample sunlight. Throughout the ordeal of being stung and harassed by Ernest's bees, the beautiful purple rhododendrons in the sunlight became my point of focus. I would hand my pain, my stress and my frustration over to their blossoms. They became a form of higher power that helped me through the stress of being in that laboratory. If I felt an excruciating sting, or experienced the urge to scream into the hand dryer, my gaze would instead focus on the delicate purple petals of the rhododendron. They were a meditative calming light at the end of a dark tunnel – fragile, fluttering like handcrafted paper in a secret diary, their bright orange stamens standing erect and powdered with pollen. The bees, too, would give their attention to the rhododendrons, buzzing in and out, hungrily collecting nectar and returning to the hive outside the window. This simple act of bee behaviour allowed me to have compassion for them. I felt an empathic union with them. We both depended on the rhododendrons to get by.

Alas, if I am to be candid, I must admit I would sometimes fantasise about harming the bees; I would imagine smashing them under my fist. But this would have been wrong and cruel. They were simply being bees, collecting pollen and surviving. If I took their stings personally, then I would have failed as a biologist. Ernest Kinsella, however, should have done better. He should not have prioritised the recreation of his bees above my safety and emotional stability. They did not need to be given freedom of the laboratory. I can see this now, but back then I was young and I didn't have the confidence to assert myself. It was immature of me to want to harm the bees, but I must also forgive myself for these urges, which caused me great shame at the time.

It was this shame, however, that made it decidedly hurtful when Ernest Kinsella first accused me of killing several of his bees. From mid-September 2008, each of his eight colonies had begun to drop in number at a rate of more than two hundred bees a day. This behaviour was bizarre within apiculture, as Ernest would furiously inform me. There was no logical cause for worker bees to abandon a queen: it simply did not happen. For Ernest, the only possible explanation was that I, through an act of utterly unprofessional contempt, had been method-ically killing his bees and hiding their corpses. I pleaded my innocence through tears, which infuriated the remaining bees and caused them to sting my lips. I assured him that, while I was admittedly indignant about sharing a lab with untethered bees, I would never descend to such boorish conduct. But this was not enough. Ernest raised hue and cried to the academic authorities of our institution. They believed him. I was ordered to move out of the laboratory with immediate effect and was given, instead, access to a common lab in another building on campus, which was insufficient for my mollusc research. Frankly, I was thankful that I wasn't expelled outright, so did not protest. In a final act of spite, Ernest informally appointed himself as the custodian of my rhododendrons, and refused me their possession. He argued that the bees were too fond of them and that to remove the flowers would distress them further. This proved to be an unwise decision on his part.

That was to be the last time I ever spoke to or saw Ernest Kinsella. His bees continued to disappear at an increasing rate over the weeks that followed. There was no evidence of death, no evidence of sickness or dying. The bees simply went away, and eventually only the queen was left. Then she, too, disappeared. The melittology department was stumped. Consultants were brought in from other universities to pore over Kinsella's research. They tested for chemicals in the colonies, for viruses too. They studied CCTV footage of the hives. One thing was certain, however: my innocence was proven. I had not been harming or killing the bees during my time sharing the lab with Ernest. As they continued to disappear after I left, this ruled me out. Instead, foul play was suspected on Kinsella's part. I am certain this would have been very hurtful to him. I did not receive an apology from Kinsella or the institution, although I now forgive him. I am sure the anguish of losing his bees and his PhD was of greater concern than my feelings.

Readers conversant with apiculture or melittology will be aware that the disappearance of Ernest Kinsella's bees in Geneva was the first scientifically recorded incident of colony collapse disorder, where an otherwise healthy population of worker bees will abandon their queen and food supply for no discernible reason – a phenomenon that is now happening worldwide at an exponential rate, with dangerous consequences for biodiversity and crop pollination. Sadly, Ernest Kinsella himself disappeared in October 2008. It is not known precisely what happened to him, although it is generally accepted that the profound stress of the entire situation caused him to take his own life.

Towards a theory

I have recounted these events over and over in my mind for several years. I am not at all satisfied with the current accepted explanations for the collapse of Kinsella's colony, or for colony collapse disorder in general, or for the disappearance of Ernest Kinsella. I believe that there is an alternative explanation, which I will outline thus.

I surmise that the unifying factor in the disappearance of both Kinsella's bees and Kinsella himself is the *Rhododendron ponticum* that sat in the vase in the laboratory. I experienced the flower to be beautiful and transfixing, as previously mentioned, but I also felt a strange draw to it, as if it were calling me or pulling me in. The experience could be described as spiritual, in a sense. The carpel area of this particular rhododendron had a magnetism to it, like shimmering heat rising from hot tarmac, which set it apart from other blooms.

I contacted Roy Stunt in 2014 with questions pertaining to the particular rhododendrons he had gifted me for my twenty-third birthday, the ones I had kept in the vase in the lab. I wanted to know as much as possible about the species and the area from which they had been picked.

Roy informed me that he had been investigating the invasion of rhododendrons in the Meyrin area of Geneva – the species had taken an aggressive position within meadows there and was threatening natural biodiversity. In fact, out of all the blooms in the Meyrin area, *Rhododendron ponticum* was the most prevalent. The flowers that Roy gifted me were from this particular batch, picked in September 2008.

Readers with a knowledge of physics will be aware of the significance of both the time and location of the extraction of this rhododendron sample. Geneva, specifically the Meyrin area, is home to CERN and the Large Hadron Collider (LHC). Now, this field is by no means my area of competence – I have but an elementary knowledge of particle physics. I am also conscious of the scepticism of the general scientific community regarding cross-disciplinary hypotheses. But I will attempt a brief explanation nonetheless.

The LHC is an enormous device. It is a particle accelerator. This means that physicists use the LHC to smash subatomic particles against each other and then measure the results of those collisions. To put it crudely, they try to recreate the exact moments after the Big Bang, which is theorised to be the singular event in which all reality and the universe were created, billions of years ago.

The LHC was first started up on 10 September 2008. Leading up to this, there were many years of fear and debate around the safety of this operation. These debates played out in both the scientific community and the media. Professor Otto Rössler, a German chemist at the Eberhard Karls University of Tübingen, was the most vocal opponent of the LHC and attempted to block it from ever being turned on by bringing an application to the European Court of Human Rights. The professor stated in 2008:

CERN itself has admitted that mini black holes could be created when the particles collide, but they don't consider this a risk.

My own calculations have shown that it is quite plausible that these little black holes survive and will grow exponentially and eat the planet from the inside. I have been calling for CERN to hold a safety conference to prove my conclusions wrong but they have not been willing.

Professor Rössler was ignored. Not only was he ignored, but his fears of the LHC creating black holes that would consume all of reality were also proven wrong. A black hole, for those unfamiliar, is a region of space whose gravitational pull is such that no light or radiation can escape it. Nothing can exist in a black hole, not even time. Large stars, much more massive than our sun, eventually expand and collapse on themselves to become black holes. The LHC has been in regular operation for more than ten years now, and here we are, safe and sound. It has led to many important discoveries, most notably the existence of the Higgs boson, or 'God particle', in 2012. The LHC has been a resounding success in particle physics and has proven itself to be safe to operate – this statement receives almost unanimous agreement. I disagree, and must revisit Professor Rössler's fears within a new context.

It is my strong belief that on the morning of 10 September 2008, when the LHC was first turned on and the particles within collided, the machine emitted a localised blast of Hawking radiation, which is the specific type of radiation theorised to be emitted by black holes. Hawking radiation is particularly sensitive to light that has a wavelength of between 380 and 450 nanometres on the light spectrum. In layperson's terms, this is visible light that the human eye experiences as the colour purple or violet.

Growing near the LHC in the meadows of Meyrin were several invasive specimens of *Rhododendron ponticum*. Analysis of their petals will show that they are precisely 410 nanometres on the light spectrum. They are a very pure and definite purple. These rhododendrons, due to their colouring, thus absorbed significant amounts of Hawking radiation on the morning of 10 September 2008.

If, as my calculations predict, this was the case, it would, as per Professor Rössler's fears, explain why we have not seen the creation of black holes or had all reality consumed. The rhododendrons protected the Earth from the creation of a destructive black hole. However, their absorption of Hawking radiation led to the creation of many localised black holes, existing exclusively within the pistils at the centres of the rhododendrons present in Meyrin.

Unified theory for CCD

I posit that the rhododendrons gifted to me by the botanist Roy Stunt contained black holes within their centres.

I posit that their mesmeric, calming quality was, in fact, the presence of Hawking radiation.

And I posit that the flowers on my desk consumed any visiting bees via their black holes, possibly via a currently unrecorded process of reversible evanescence.

I infer this claim on the likely emission of Hawking radiation from the LHC and its sensitivity to the specific colour of purple present in *Rhododendron ponticum*.

If this position is correct, the bees in Kinsella's colony were each consumed by miniature black holes situated within the centre of the rhododendrons while they attempted to collect pollen. This explains why there was no evidence of death or no observable pattern of migration. It also offers an explanation for the mesmerising quality that I personally observed while staring at the flowers. I was observing Hawking radiation expelled from bees that had passed the event horizon of the black holes.

This axiom coincides with the aggressiveness with which *Rhododendron ponticum* has spread worldwide as an invasive plant species since 2008. The Hawking radiation altered the genetics of the plants that were on my desk and any other specimens in the Meyrin area in September 2008 so that any offspring would seed with black holes at their centres. I believe that almost all specimens of this plant have since been 'infected' with black holes due to bee pollination. Not all bees are sucked into the black holes – some safely collect pollen from the stamen and successfully fertilise other plants of the species. It is the bees who pass the event horizon, situated in the pistil, that disappear into the flower's black hole.

These mutated rhododendrons have a distinct advantage over any contesting plants in their environment, as they benefit from being pollinated while also consuming bees before they can pollinate competing species, thus aggressively reducing floral biodiversity to a monoculture of *Rhododendron ponticum*.

Where have all the bees gone?
Under an Einsteinian interpretation of gravity, it is understood that a black hole is all-consuming and destructive. However, the existence of Loop Quantum Gravity (LQG), as posited by Singh and Almado of Louisiana State University in 2018, argues otherwise. Under this interpretation, a black hole is not a destructive singularity but rather a type of portal. What is on the

other side of this portal is unknown, but it has been theorised that it may be an instance of time, past or future, or interdimensional: a separate plane of reality.

I am, with the weight of my professional career and Nobel prize on the line, suggesting to the scientific community through this letter to *The Irish Times* today that the world's bees are disappearing into miniature black holes situated within the pistils of a genetically mutated species of *Rhododendron ponticum*, and that this explains the widespread phenomenon of colony collapse disorder. I believe that LQG is allowing bees, not to die, but to disappear to either another point in time or a separate dimension of reality. This is where all the bees have gone.

This situation could have devastating effects, in particular, if the bees are travelling to a point in the historic past that predated their evolution. If modern bees, for instance, were travelling to the Paleozoic period, approximately 500 million years ago, or to a point during the Cambrian explosion, their advanced evolution would give them a distinct upper hand over the insects in existence at that time. Were they to travel to the Cretaceous or Jurassic periods, they could even sting dinosaurs in the face. While I acknowledge that certain elements of the previous paragraph and most of the following may constitute unscientific alarmist conjecture on my part, I nonetheless feel a responsibly to share my anxieties.

These bees may be capable of altering events happening in the present, without us even being aware, and could change the nature of life on Earth as we know it. I recently shared this fear with my learned colleague Professor Dennis Foreword, who suggested another chilling possibility. In the event of an interdimensional explanation, bees could be using rhododendrons to travel to what we understand to be the 'afterlife', or spiritual realm, populated by human souls – meaning our deceased loved ones are being tormented by aggressive stinging bees who have been displaced from their plane of existence.

The disappearance of Ernest Kinsella

Of personal concern to me, and no doubt his loved ones, is the disappearance of Ernest. I do not believe that he took his own life. No suicide note was left; no friends suggested that he was behaving differently.

I believe that Ernest Kinsella was stung by one of his own bees, which had travelled into a rhododendron's black hole and then successfully returned from the portal. I suggest we call these hypothetical creatures 'quantum bees'. It is possible that regular bees, via exposure to intense Hawking radiation present at the event horizon, can sting a human being, and that the site of this sting can become a black hole. This means that Kinsella could have been sucked into a hole in his own arm, causing him to travel to a point in time or a separate dimension. And it is possible that this occurrence is becoming quite common. I base this on the wider phenomenon of species extinction on Earth, which has rapidly accelerated in recent years.

Towards a collapse of biodiversity and mass species extinction

If a small percentage of consumed bees are returning from rhododendron black holes as quantum bees with an enhanced ability to sting black holes into any creature they attack, then this offers a viable explanation for not only disappearing humans, but also the mass extinctions currently befalling insects, mammals and vertebrates on Earth.

Global warming is not causing mass extinctions. Instead, creatures worldwide are being stung by quantum bees. The afflicted creature simply turns inside out and is sucked into the site of the sting on their bodies.

Immediate action/solution/prevention

As outlined above, two possibilities exist. Bees and any lifeforms capable of being stung by a bee are disappearing. They are relocating to either a point in time, past or future, or a separate dimension of reality. Both possibilities are cause for alarm in our present reality on earth.

While global warming is definitely real – I will not argue against the evidence – its position as the great threat it is currently believed to be is exaggerated and harmful. Global warming is not causing colony collapse disorder in bees, or a collapse in biodiversity within plants and insects, or mass extinctions of mammals. Billions in funds and human labour is being misdirected towards the halting of global warming, a practice that, I warn you, is in vain and must stop.

The first action required is the complete and immediate eradication of all specimens of *Rhododendron ponticum*. This particular species has become invasive and widespread in temperate areas across Europe, Asia and America. We must assume that, due to the presence of colony collapse disorder in bees, these plants also contain black holes. This effort will require global cooperation and diplomacy. I would be willing to lead this endeavour.

The Large Hadron Collider must cease operations. Its continued emission of Hawking radiation have likely further caused black holes to appear in rhododendrons. Of great worry is the possibility that any purple-coloured flower or object may have been 'infected' with black holes, due to the sensitivity of Hawking radiation on this spectrum. We, as a society, should eradicate the colour purple as a precautionary measure. Any purple plant, object or animal should be humanely dispatched, or at the very least painted over or dyed a different colour to prevent Hawking radiation sensitivity. We must adjust to a world where the colour purple does not exist until biodiversity is restored.

Funded expedition

The above procedures are recommendations to attempt to prevent any further disappearance of Earth's life forms – to prevent and eradicate the appearance of miniature black holes only. This does not, however, offer a possibility for the safe return to this reality of other lifeforms that have travelled via the black holes present in rhododendrons or at the sites of quantum bee stings.

The only way to find out if a return is possible is for a team of humans to attempt to travel to the other side of these black holes. It is scientifically impossible to shrink humans to the size of a bee to enable them to travel via a rhododendron black hole, but there may be a possible route via a sting by a quantum bee.

Logic dictates that when a human is stung, and the site of this sting creates a black hole, the human is then sucked into a black hole on their own body. This would cause the human or animal body to turn inside out while it engages in interdimensional travel. We must assume that the humans and animals who have travelled via black holes are capable of existing in whatever plane or time or reality they travel to. Otherwise, quantum bees could not return to this reality to sting us in the first place. But these mammals on the other side of black holes most likely exist with their internal organs on the outsides of their bodies, and this form of mutilation must be a perfectly safe mode of existence on the other side. Bees, in this reality, have exoskeletons, so their skeletons become internal when they enter the rhododendron event horizons.

I require a team of scientists who will volunteer to have their bodies surgically turned inside out – their bones, lungs and guts on the outside; their mouths, noses, eyes and genitals on the outside too. With life-support equipment and a sterile environment, it would be possible to keep a human alive in this state for twenty-four hours. It would, however, be extremely painful.

I would use this window to sting the inside-out scientists with quantum bees. The scientists would thus be sucked into a black hole on their inside-out bodies. However, they would find themselves no longer inside out on the opposite side of the black hole, and thus capable of recording and analysing the interdimensional environment to where all of Earth's lifeforms are disappearing. The scientists would hopefully then return to this dimension inside out by stinging themselves with a quantum bee, leaving another small window here, to surgically turn them right side in.

I urge that this approach be considered for the future of life on this planet. On a personal level, I would like to inquire as to the possibility of returning Ernest Kinsella, who I believe exists inside out in another dimension. He is deserving of recognition as the world's first human to engage in interdimensional travel.

Yours sincerely,

Dr Marie Gaffney

Gary Sinise — Wikipedia
Wikipedia wiki?

gary
sinise x3

Fuck
ISIS

THE GIANTS OF THE GALTEE MOUNTAINS

Art Ó Laoire is crying on his front porch because Mr Gosling is kicking his da in the temple. Now Mr Goff is there too. He's telling Art to go back inside, but then he starts to punch his father in the head while Mr Gosling holds his shoulders down on the driveway. There's a queue of children at the ice-cream van, but Podge the Dolphin isn't serving them because he's watching Fintan Ó Laoire get a bateing off the other das. This is all happening because I started wanking last month and can't stop.

Granda Jerry is a cheapskate. All the other lads went to Trabolgan for mad craic in the summer, when the pool was open, when the crowds were buzzing the place. But not me. We went to Trabolgan in September, when the cold came upon it, and the leaves started to yellow, and there were no lifesavers, no students on part-time jobs in those orange T-shirts with limp collars that give anyone who wears them a set of bitch tits. No burger vans, no warmth, no sun, just squeezing days and the purgatorial bang of abandonment.

What's Trabolgan? Only the most class holiday village down at the bottom of Cork on the arse-end of an ocean inlet. If you could look straight ahead, long enough into the distance from that south coast, with curvy eyes on you, you'd see Antarctica. It has all the usual holiday village business you'd want to be getting up to. You could spend a day on the mini-cars, battering into the backs of other lads, pure Mario Kart, real petrol engines blaring like a throat. Go mad on ice cream too.

The best thing about Trabolgan is the ice cream. You know the way when you go up to an ice-cream van at home on your estate and they have all those pictures of multicoloured cones in the back beside the machine? Green ice-cream cones, or ones with caramel veins swirling through them? Or the ice-cream cone that pushes straight out of the machine, and then gets dipped in melted chocolate, and the chocolate freezes solid, so when you bite into the cone you're cracking through a thin chocolate meniscus? But when you ask for them off the van that drives into your estate, they never fucking have them? Just a regular cone or a 99, maybe a bit of raspberry syrup, if even. They never have all the different variations that they actually advertise. Well, down in Trabolgan they do have them. The ice-cream vans dip the cones in melted chocolate. And it hardens and develops these chocolate sweat beads when you breathe on it in the heat. They have a separate machine full of sugary mint soft-serve. They have caramel swirly cones, and mad sweet pecan nuts, and pure gobbledygook hundreds and thousands, and fucking white flakes, not the regular brown flakes, but white flakes that you stick in if you want it. Hollywood style. That's the plethora of ice-cream that the lads would be able to get down in Trabolgan.

I knew this, coz they'd fucking tell me about it. Dickie Slattery and all the boys in Douglas would rub it in my face as soon as we'd be back in school. Talking about mad-bastard ice-cream cones, and I'd be stuck back in the city, bursty hot bubbling tarmac smelling like road, no one on my estate, empty footpaths, with Podge the Dolphin hanging his big pregnant belly out over the partition of the Mr Whippy van, telling me to go fuck myself and take the 99 whenever I ordered anything fancy off his sun-bleached menu on the back wall of the van.

'Why'd you have it there if you don't sell any of those ice creams, Podge?'

And he'd say 'Fuck off you little bitch', because my hair is long, and my voice isn't broken. Eating it on my own on the curb. Everyone else down in Trabolgan, having gas craic, smoking fags, their parents off too.

One day I made Dickie Slattery cry. He was slagging me over my ice-cream poverty, so I told him that his ma got ridden by Art Ó Laoire's da over the summer. I heard off Podge the Dolphin that Art Ó Laoire's da rents the biggest holiday house in Trabolgan, the one with the conservatory beside the pitch and putt course. And big Fintan Ó Laoire has gold chains hanging down between his open shirt all year round to show off his silver chest hair. And he plies all the other das with crates of Heineken and German porn on the TV. And then he snakes out, knowing which wife is at home on her own, and he goes over and rides the wives. And Dickie Slattery's ma got ridden by Art Ó Laoire's da that summer in Trabolgan. That shut him the fuck up, when I said it out loud in front of everyone on the road, with his ice cream dipped in melty hot chocolate.

Art Ó Laoire is no different. He knows all about sex and tried to show us all his da's playing cards that had tanned men riding women who were wearing bras that have the patterns you'd see on a fancy cake or a doily. Art ruins games of soccer by bringing up shifting and handjobs and blowjobs. He tried to make me and Nessa Goff shift, and when I didn't want to he started shouting 'Hahaha, it's coz he can't cum. He hasn't even had wet dreams yet. He's a fridget,' and then Nessa looked at me like I was nothing. And I felt like nothing because I hadn't had one yet, and I hated that Art knew.

This summer I could take no more. I was done with being the only lad in Douglas who had to stay behind while everyone else went to Trabolgan. I'd wake up, and the sun would be creeping under the blinds, and it would bring a few seconds of contentment, and then an acidic little shit of a twist would grab the stomach when I'd remember that I was stuck there on the estate. Ma and Da both live in Israel coz Da has a job as a secretary with the Irish consulate. They won't let me live in Tel Aviv with them in their apartment coz at night-time the missile sirens go off, and they have to hop out of their beds and head downstairs to the shelter on the bottom floor. Ma said that if I lived there I'd develop issues with my nerves, that I'd start picking my skin again or washing my hands until they're raw. That I'm better off staying in Douglas with Granda Jerry looking after me. They have a point. I used to have these obsessions. Jerry kind of has them too. My doctor calls them 'rituals'. Where I'll get an idea in my head and I can't get it out, like thinking that Ma will die if I don't pick my skin. So I became obsessed with picking skin off my hands, and that would stop her dying in a car crash or being killed by a dog. But that type of stuff hasn't bothered me in nearly four years.

I had Trabolgan planned. I went out onto the landing, outside Jerry's bedroom, opened the ironing cupboard and walloped my head off the water heater until I knocked myself out. And Jerry came up and poured cold tea on my face, and I woke up and told him that I wanted to go to Trabolgan in August, when everybody else went there. And he told me to go sort my life out. So I did it again the next night, and the night after that, until I had a turquoise green stain on my forehead from the copper rust off the water tank, until Jerry gave in and asked Ma and Da to send over the money for a three-week holiday at the start of August.

So they did, and I was over the moon, and I went out onto the road and told Art Ó Laoire and Dickie Slattery and Nessa Goff, and they were sickened. Sickened that I'd be on the mini-cars, and flaking down the water slides, and smoking fags and giving myself American dreams with my hands around my neck. Eating two chocolate-dipped ice-cream cones, one in either hand like the Lord Mayor of Cork. But what did Granda Jerry do? He fucking kept half the money that Ma and Da sent from Israel to get a Sky dish installed. All the sports channels, all the movie channels, two-year contract. He kept half the money for himself and booked Trabolgan for 3 September like a prick.

A discount Trabolgan experience. All the rides closed, no amenities. Two grey weeks in a depressing, empty holiday village. The only good part was missing school. August passed. The unmerciful slagging I got when everyone came back in the last week of August before school, calling me a liar. 'Why weren't you in Trabolgan, Roy?' 'Telling fibs were ya, boy?' I looked like an absolute eejit, after making a show of myself with my brags. 'I'm going in September,' I'd say. 'Fucking September, no one goes in September,' they'd say.

The journey down was a tense one. Granda Jerry had the radio on, listening to loopers on Joe Duffy complaining about the price of food in cinemas, and Jerry nodding his head, talking about how he brings a bunch of bananas to the pictures out of spite. Anytime the word popcorn was mentioned on the radio, he made a little spit motion with his lips, and looked up into the rear-view mirror to catch my eye, and referred to popcorn as 'puffy Yank styrofoam for apeshits'. He did it about nine times, and there was a fume of an anger inside in me towards Granda Jerry, the tight-arse. So I reached into the back of my mouth, four fingers, and pulled at the lumpy rear of my tongue where the white fur is. The morning's Coco Pops flew out as I bent towards the back of Jerry's car seat and made sure I got as much of the hot puke down the back of his shirt as I could, and he howled. 'I'm car sick, Jerry,' I said. And he started roaring, and I felt power. We'd stopped by Cotter's Barn, and Jerry threatened to turn back, and I threatened to bang my head off the road and say he hit me. So he took off his shirt and fucked it in a ditch, and drove to Trabolgan bare-chested and cowld. He turned the radio up full blast and wore Joe Duffy's voice like a gown to keep his torso warm.

'Have we got long to go?' I asked him eventually. Because at this point, we'd gone beyond cottages and regional roads, even a quare bóithrín had been traversed. I didn't trust Jerry's judgement on the journey. He's fully liable of taking a bollocks of a detour to avoid a toll booth or a petrol station, in case I'd be asking him to stop for a can of Lucozade.

'What length is long?' he said, striking his manky silver chin stubble.

'What type of a prick's question is that, Jerry?'

'How am I to know how long is left, when I've no way to either quantify or summarise what your personal definition of long is?

Your long and my long could be two separate longs altogether. If I were to posit an answer, and I overestimated what your long was, then I'd find myself in a most terribly unfair situation. I'd be in your debt then.'

He always pulled this type of caper out of his hoop. This is why I'd my mouth shut for most of the drive.

'My long would be more than half an hour, Jerry. My short would be less than fifteen minutes.' I said that through my teeth, nearly grinding my back molars down, I felt pressure in my head because of it.

'We're twenty minutes away ta fuck, relax the britches.'

Scrunching back into the faux leather of the Cortina with the frustration coursing through my belly, I was distracted by the tang of bile rising off of Jerry's veiny shoulders, but then that was quelled by a freshness coming in from the crack in the car door with a bit of salt on the air. We were up in a pine forest that was fair near the ocean, by the feel of it. We'd been driving for the bones of two hours. 'We're almost there now', Jerry offered out of his purse gob.

After a few narrow windy lengths of road, it started to open up a bit. You could tell by the little furrows of manicured grass on the roadside that there was something worth talking about ahead. Sure as shit, the signs for Trabolgan started popping up. First it was a proper one, on a real road sign. Then smaller, private signs. Trabolgan 1km. Trabolgan Next Left. Trabolgan Just Ahead. The excitement was fizzy in me. The car met a barrier, and we stopped. 'Trabolgan Holiday Village' said the sign, and it had a map on it, with pictures of canoes and oars and stoats. There was this security hut beside the barrier, not the shit security huts you'd expect in a car park, it was more like a prefab, and you could tell that the guard probably had a fierce gas time in there. A coffee machine, a TV, a radio, his own jacks so he'd never need to leave his post. I was only imagining this, but it had the look of that type of prefab. The guard wasn't forthcoming though. You'd expect him to come out when a car arrived at the barrier, but he didn't.

Jerry went to clutch for a pearl-handled butter knife that he kept in the small leather compartment behind the gear stick. His car door was broken, and you could only open it by jamming a thin piece of metal into the locking mechanism. He'd it worn down to the point that it couldn't be fixed, and even he wanted to pay to get it fixed. Which was a drastic state of affairs, even by his Fagan logic.

I watched him leave, bare-chested, with the olive spots spat all over his leathery back. He'd the look of one of those birds that are weak from an oil spill on a beach that you'd see on the news. Coming towards us on the opposite side of the road was a red Toyota hatchback. It was all packed up with a roof-rack full of suitcases. The man in the car reached out over the passenger window and stuck his ticket into the tangerine-coloured box that lifted the barrier. Granda Jerry stopped in front of the offending car. There was a family in there, two lads around my own age and a ma. Jerry was roaring something, I couldn't hear what, probably asking where the security guard was to let us in. But whatever he was asking, it made the man beep his horn over and over and rev his engine. The car nearly went for Jerry, and he'd to back out of the way. It was then that I noticed he still had the butter knife in his fist. No wonder the family almost rolled him over. Some ould lad bare-chested at the barrier holding a fucking knife? Are you for real, Jerry? They must have thought he was an escaped lunatic.

As the car revved past, from the back seat I could see the look of satiation in the gape of the two lads inside. They'd had an entire August of the summer camp. All the joy in the world, their eyes as full as bellies with mad excitement. The youngest with strawberry blond hair caught my own eyeline. I could sense his contempt. I felt my jealousy as a ball of fire behind my nose. He knew well what we were up to. He could see it in the mood of our broken Cortina that we were tight-arses, coming to Trabolgan on the cheap when it's empty. The shame upon me was swampy. I was a tight-arse, inherited tight-arsedness off my granda. I wanted to tell them this. It wasn't fair. 'Probably Yank spastics,' Jerry howled after them.

With all the commotion off of Jerry's lungs, the security guard emerged from behind his hut, a tall lad of about thirty. He walked towards the barrier to Jerry, his gait slow and suspicious, one hand close to his chest, as if he was ready to radio the guards from the device on his collar. I could see his name tag, it said Paul. Jerry got jittery with the sight of the guard and let out a few words. 'I've a summer home booked inside for myself and the young lad. Are ye going to let us in at all? Or will I be wasting a tenner's petrol in the car while I have it running at that barrier? An engine does fine gulping in neutral, like.'

There was a pause of caution out of the security guard. As he got closer to him, he saw the butter knife and bare chest. His apprehension settled into a more authoritative demeanour when he noticed that Jerry was in his seventies.

'Have you ID?' he said.

'I've an ID of getting past this barrier,' said Jerry.

There was a pause, Jerry sucked his top lip and clenched an eye 'cause he'd said something witty.

'Stay there another minute and I'll be out to ye again.'

Jerry sauntered back to the car and chucked the butter knife on the front seat. There was a September lick coming in my window, the type that had a bite of cowld on it, the type that lets you know that summer has just finished.

'Put your shirt back on,' I said to him.

'It's beyond below in a ditch, I sacrificed it,' he said with a poor mouth on him.

'Take my T-shirt. It's better for me to be bare-chested and you to be clothed. You're the adult.' I snarled that like Ma would, and I felt big.

'It's not. That's worse. Are you stone mad? It'll look like I'm in a belly top with a bare-chested child.'

'Then at least wipe the sick off.'

'I'd have to be rubbing myself off the grass like I'm a pair of shoes covered in dog shit, boy. Watch now, I'll get him to throw in a few goodies for the summer house.'

It became clear to me with that comment that the butter knife and bare chest were part of a theatrical ruse. A type of bemused intimidation, to make himself so spectacularly and shamelessly bizarre that another person would just bend to his requests to escape how uncomfortable they felt in his presence. To make poor ould Paul nervous and self-conscious. Jerry was all about spectacle, the shock of the spectacle as a technique to coerce others into his own will. Paul came out with an envelope.

'Ye're in house number 238, up above a hill, fine courtyard, ye're only a few minutes' walk from the leisure centre.'

'And you'll be down with a few basics, you will?' said Jerry with a squint eye. 'You'll come down with a few litres of milk? Or a skelp of butter or a few loaves of bread? You will?'

'I will.' There was a defeated tremble in the security lad's throat when he said that.

The barrier lifted and we drove into Trabolgan towards the houses. Several cars passed us in the opposite direction, the last families in exodus, going back to their regular lives, their jobs, their classrooms. A few hundred metres down, my worst fear was approaching us – little white rectangle on wheels, looming larger on the horizon as it got closer. It was the fucking Mr Whippy ice-cream van, with its American flags all taped up and its windows closed. Leaving with my one hope of getting a chocolate-dipped soft-serve cone. A loneliness came upon me.

The summer home was a harsh box, watery porridge pebble-dash on the outside walls. It was the bulb off a normal suburban house but it was about six inches short in every direction. The door frames, the windows, the radiators, all very familiar, but slightly dwarfed. Everything was a simulation of a family home, but with a bang of distrust. I know it sounds mad to say that a building doesn't trust you, but this gaff didn't trust us. The windows opened out half way so you'd never fall out. The hairdryer, the toaster, the microwave, the trouser press ... no plugs. Everything was mainlined into the walls like veins. The house was a pulsing body. It had an immune system. The houses were a fake playhouse version of the suburban houses that people left to holiday here in the first place. Fucking madness. The bricks in the walls watched with square eyes the bedlam that people came here for. These abodes were not intended to be lived in but stayed in, for short bursts. They were your host.

Granda Jerry started drinking Tesco lager. He said the water heater was just a fat-bastard kettle that sounded like one of the giants of the Galtee Mountains crying over their dead wife under a hedge when you turned it on. I could see his point. I'd never come across a more aggressively efficient water heater. Outside the window, big hot steamy white ballsack plumes rose up and would burn the wrist of anyone upstairs if they happened to stick their arm out the jacks window at the same time that you had the steam on. Jerry drank cans and went wild with the water heater, turning it on full blast just for the sake of it. 'Are you watching this?' he'd say. He was happy. 'Have you any idea how uneconomical this would be if we were paying per use, lad? You couldn't have a heater like this in a regular house. You'd end up in a debtor's prison before you'd the hairs on your arse washed.'

Jerry once wrote a play called *The Giants of the Galtee Mountains*. It was about a cult of giants in the Galtee Mountains who'd correctly predicted the assassination of JFK two years before it happened. The play never made it as far as a stage, and you could never mention it around Jerry or he'd get a fit of anger. But with drink on him, it was different. With drink, the play was all he wanted to talk about. He'd compare everything around him to the giants of the Galtee Mountains. He'd start off kind of proud or cocky, like the person listening should know what a giant from the Galtee Mountains was, but then he'd get this sadness in his eyes that looked like he had a secret pain in his belly that he didn't want to talk about. Sometimes, with enough drink in him, Jerry would move the couches out of the living room in the house back home, and he'd use the space as a little stage where he'd perform the show, on his own, playing every character.

When I was younger, like nine or ten, he'd make me watch, and I felt so embarrassed for him that it gave me stomach ulcers and there was blood in my shits. Ma and Da banned any performances of *The Giants of the Galtee Mountains* from the house after that.

Jerry looked at his reflection in the kitchen window of our Trabolgan chalet. When he's drunk, for some reason, the stubble on his face looks longer. He said that the drink dehydrates his face, so his skin shrinks a bit and the hair only *looks* longer, like on corpses. He turned on the dishwasher with no dishes in it, and opened it mid-cycle, and the kitchen filled with steam and he said, 'Do you see this dishwasher? When I open it, it's like one of the giants of the Galtee Mountains yawning.' I refused to entertain this, out of spite. He tried to give me a can of Tesco lager. I said, 'No.' He said, 'That's the best part of a bob, that is. I'm being generous, stay up and have a sup. Who are you to refuse that? Fucking Robert Maxwell, is it?' I went to bed.

My bedroom had those big-breeze block slabs on the wall painted with magnolia emulsion, like the changing room in the gym in school. They had puckered impressions in them. My bed farted faint rubber squeaks when I turned over; it had a piss-proof undercover on the mattress.

I was aware that sleeping in a new bed and room can feel weird. It's just because it's different to what I'm used to, and I knew it would bring scary dreams. But I was also very tired from the day. I tried to think of boring things from my room at home. Like my door handle, or the Lucozade stain on my carpet that looks like Italy. But the dreams still came. I was on a roof. It was a hot night with these yellow sparks that jumped in the dark towards my eyes and bounced off my skin, and I swear I felt the stings in my bed. And I was in Israel crying. Ma and Da's apartment was burning, so I went inside. John Fitzgerald Kennedy wore a gas mask and the top of his forehead was missing, and then he was helping Pontius Pilate pick snooker balls out of the hedge behind O'Donovan's butchers. Da's face was melting, with flames running down his chin. And I could smell burning plastic. And when Da tried to speak, blue flames dripped to the ground, and they made a zipping noise as they fell. The way a melted plastic toy soldier zips on the end of a hot poker in front of the fireplace. And Da's eyeballs bulged out, bulging with my heartbeat, in and out of the sockets with a sucky noise. Ma was engulfed in this purple flame. She was calm, hunched over, but I could see the white bones of her ribcage.

I woke up famished for breath, with a very lonesome thud in my chest. And then that rare joy that only happens when you realise it was a dream and not real life. The peach glow of light outside the house crept in, enough to cast rectangle shadows on the breeze-block walls, and I remembered that I wasn't at home in my own bed back in Douglas. I thought about Ma and Da in Israel. My pyjama pants were hot wet, as if the rubber undersheet had prompted me to piss myself. But it wasn't piss, it was cum. It smelled like pasta. This was a wet dream. I'd pretended to all the lads in school that I'd had wet dreams, and pretended that I'd wanked. But I hadn't, and I'd started to feel a bit nervous that I hadn't. Like I was never going to be able to cum and I'd just have to pretend that I could cum for the rest of my life, and if I ever had to have sex with a girl I'd have to piss inside her so she'd think I could cum. I washed my jocks in the Trabolgan shower. The water was hot, and then cold, and then hot again. Jerry was still awake in the kitchen, turning the water heater on and off, drinking, thinking about the giants of the Galtee Mountains. I felt like a man.

The morning had a dampness, the type that rots leaves and wood, and tells bees to go away and die. The sound of my footsteps came back at me as I explored the roads of the weird houses. Sure as fuck. Empty. We were the only family in Trabolgan. There were only a handful of staff still working. Mostly caretakers and gardeners. They thought I was Polish, and that myself and Jerry came to Trabolgan in September because we couldn't read the brochures. It was getting cold. Jerry took day trips to Tesco for cans. The bar by the pool was closed until the following June. There was a lad called Jordan working as a caretaker who felt a bit sorry for me, because he fired up the go-karts for my sole use. And I would bate around the track on my own. Hopping off nothing, only the cunts in my head. Bateing off the back of Dickie Slattery and Nessa Goff. Laughing at them. And I imagined seeing Nessa's thighs in her bicycle shorts, and I got hard, and I could feel the vibration of the kart seat travel up my arse, and it made me harder, so I'd try and hide the bulge in my fist, and squeeze it real firmly, and do laps and laps of the go-kart track, and Jordan watched.

Most days I'd just soak in the TV. I got bored of the go-karts. Trabolgan was purgatory, the caretakers and gardeners ignored me. It was getting colder and it was raining a lot. I'd call down to Paul the security guard in his daycent prefab hut. He only ever wanted to talk about Manchester United and their chances this season. I know nothing about soccer but Paul didn't care, he'd just list out men's second names and either praise or curse them. Paul had a tattoo of Bugs Bunny in a wheelchair smoking a bong. It was on his belly. He said he got it 'cause he lost a bet in Barcelona on a stag.

He told me about hooers in Barcelona. He told me that he'd say to his wife that he was going to Barcelona for a long weekend to buy racing pigeons. But really, him and his best friend Tulip were going over for hooers. He said that Romanian hooers are the best. That you can tell where their brothels are because an ould one with cleavage will come up talking to you if you're having a pint, and they'll take you to the younger ones, and they've huge brown paraffin-oil barrel arses and florescent yellow thongs the colour of a hi-vis jacket. Tulip had a threesome, and one of them washed her fanny in a sink in front of him beforehand, and he didn't have to wear a condom if he paid them an extra €50. Sometimes, when he'd go into real detail like that, my face would feel red, and I'd just look down at my shoes. I didn't really want to hear any of these stories. They made me frightened about the idea of ever having sex – but I liked them at the same time. Paul didn't seem to care, because when he got into the specifics of sex with the hooers, he didn't look at me. Instead he'd tell the stories to this framed photograph of Alex Ferguson that was on the prefab wall. The sex talk only ever stopped when he'd eventually say that he could never do things like that with his wife because she was too nice to have those things done to her, and because her father is a sound man over pints. Then he'd start talking about soccer again for a bit.

The conversations with Paul would always end in me going back to the bedroom and wanking. I'd tell Jerry I was tired, in need of a nap, and then I'd lock the door and climb into bed and pull myself asunder. I fucking loved it, but Jerry being in the same house, hearing him through a wall, drunk, roaring about the giants of the Galtee Mountains ultimately sullied the quality of the wank. I didn't give two shites about being in Trabolgan anymore. The Trabolgan bragging rights meant fuck all to me, as soon as I discovered the joys of wanking. I could hardly comprehend that it was free of charge, I marvelled at performing this act on myself. It feels, for one tiny second, like God blows on every single nerve on my body, inside and out. They should tell us about it in religion class. They should tell us about it in economics, in Irish, in history, in science class. Wanking is the first taste of an ice-cream cone, the heartbeat tug of a go-kart, the drag of a fag end. Wanking was all of these things, together and separate, magnified, boiled, distilled, expanded.

After a few days, Paul's sex stories stopped making my face go red. I'd call to his prefab just to hear them. He'd talk about double dildos, and cream pies. He told me what anal beads were, because he didn't know what they were when a hooer first had them in her and he tried to pull them like he was starting a petrol lawnmower. Then he laughed at Alex Ferguson like Alex Ferguson could laugh back.

Paul had a large black safe in his prefab, bigger than him, full of keys. His head was forever stuck into the little portable TV he had. Distracted. So I swiped the keys. And I entered every house in Trabolgan, every one of them, and I climbed into a bed in each house, and I got fully naked, and I wanked. I wanked about Nessa Goff. I wanked about the Romanian hooers in Barcelona. With the rain outside splattering on the window like grease, dripping down, and the cold of the unoccupied houses making no difference to me under the covers. Paul figured out what I was up to after a few days. I think he related to it on a nostalgic level. 'I'm down to one a day myself,' he said. 'You must be interfering with yourself like a sparky at a damp fuse box, are you? You'll get spots on your chin if you're not careful though, that happened my cousin. Ration them out.' Paul couldn't have cared less what I used the houses for as long as I didn't do a Granda Jerry on the water heaters. I did in my fuck ration them out either.

There was one house though, down by the pitch and putt course, and no key fit into it. I tried them all, and this house wouldn't open for me. I asked Paul.

'That's rented out all year,' he said. 'A man by the go of Fintan Ó Laoire has it on a long-term let. He's draped in all manner of quare dirt. He'd be doing all sorts the odd weekend in that house.'

'Doing dirtier things than you and Tulip did in Barcelona?' I said, sort of innocently.

His mouth opened, like he couldn't think of what to say next.

'Number one: what I do in Barcelona isn't that bad. Number two: you're breaking the biggest rule of the man code. Just because a man tells another man stories about Barcelona, doesn't give the other man licence to bring it up, especially out loud.'

I felt confused by this, because he'd told me that the biggest rule of the man code was to never look another man in the eye during a devil's threesome. He moved the subject matter back to Fintan Ó Laoire.

'But that lad, the lad with the house by the pitch and putt? All sorts. He'd be kicked out of Barcelona. Lad, he'd be kicked out of Portugal. Nothing out of him would be surprising me. He's hardly there most of the year but I don't even have a key to that one myself, bud.'

I wasn't disappointed, I was driven. At about seven o'clock in the morning, the damp nippy air had a sparkly glimmer on the tarmac, like when the ice cream from the fridge is too cold, so you've to let it melt a small bit for the crystals to go away. I took the pearl-handled butter knife from Jerry's car, and I forced it into the lock on the side window of Fintan Ó Laoire's house to pop it out. The place wasn't like the other houses in the holiday village. It had more space. There were bay windows by the porch for letting in light, there were extra bathrooms, there was a conservatory. It wasn't anxious or untrustworthy like the other gaffs. It had a lived-in feel. Big posh walls full of spirits trailing off into cupboards filled with tins of tomatoes and chickpeas. There were stacks of tapes in the wardrobe. I knew what they were too. Fintan was Art Ó Laoire's da, the rider of wives. These had to be tapes full of dirt.

Fintan's living room was fully decked out. White leather couch and all. He had a 28-inch television and a video recorder. I shoved the first tape into the VHS, *German Piss Witches*, it was all these German women, and they were drinking other people's piss off plates. I didn't understand why they would do that. It ruined all the bits with the sex. And there was another one called *BootyPest* that had a red-haired woman who was riding a man on a traffic roundabout and a fly landed on her arse.

I'd been getting up early, before Jerry, telling him I was off looking for racing pigeons among the wild flocks in the car park. He didn't care. Jerry was hitting the drink. I think he was driving to the Tesco drunk to get drink. I knew by the way he had the living-room seats moved towards the kitchen that he had made it into a little stage, and he was recreating his play *The Giants of the Galtee Mountains*. I think he felt he was allowed to do it in Trabolgan because Trabolgan wasn't back home. I was going straight to Fintan's house every day and climbing in the window. I wasn't even visiting Paul anymore. I'd gone through the German and Eastern European tapes several times over. I could recount every scene to you in detail. I'd it all burned into my mind.

I was rooting back in Fintan's wardrobe when I found another tape, separate from the rest, behind a shoebox with new Timberland boots in it. This tape was clearly not the same as the German ones. It was plain and black, but the words 'Do never tape over' were scraped into the plastic with a compass. I threw it into the player, the room lit up all blue, the picture fuzzy. I could make out on the screen that I was watching the very couch I was sitting on now. In my place was Martina Goff, Nessa's ma. She was wearing only a bra. She was drinking Lambrini from the bottle. I knew by the body language on Mrs Goff that she wasn't OK with the camera being there but was doing it anyway. A light from a dirty lampshade made her skin look red. She was talking about her husband Ollie. Saying that it'd break his heart if he knew she was there. Like Jupiter eclipsing a smaller planet, Fintan stepped into frame in these tiny jocks, the lamplight overexposing his belly. He looked celestial.

'Ollie doesn't appreciate the likes of you, Martina,' he said. 'Your velvet curls, the youth behind your eyes, Ollie doesn't deserve you. Ollie's off drinking down below in the bar with all the other eejits. If he'd any sense he wouldn't be letting you out of the bed. You're fierce wasted on him, doll.'

A weakness came over her face. You could tell that she hadn't received a compliment in a good stretch, and she'd nare a clue what to do with it. Fintan docked his body mass towards Mrs Goff and clutched her cheek, which caused her lips to purse forward, his rose gold bracelet clinking off her chin made patty sounds among the mushy noise of mouths. I smelled the two of them in my head, they smelled of ham. Fizzed light flickered through the blond curls of his mullet around his purple neck, a drooling golden rat. He was kissing pure deep, lounging his tongue around her gob and you could see his mickey bubbling up rubbery inside in his bitch jocks. He hauled in his stomach while Mrs Goff gave him a suckjob. It didn't look like the suckjobs on the German tapes; she was clutching his langer like it was a microphone and it looked like she was singing into it. Then they did doggy-style sex on the couch. And Fintan made guttural puffing whoops from his throat like he was choking on a dinner of chips, and Mrs Goff said, 'Oh Jesus Christ, oh Jesus Christ, oh Jesus Christ,' the whole time, non-stop.

It was awkward, they both looked like oily skin slabs. Fintan left the room as soon as he came, and the last seven minutes was just Mrs Goff, staring off into space with her eye make-up all down her nose, and the noise of the tape hissed and hummed so loud against her silence, until Fintan came back in frame with his clothes on, saying, 'You'd want to be making tracks soon enough or Ollie will start asking questions.'

I went through the rest of the tape. Nearly everyone's ma in the estate was on it. Dickie Slattery's ma, Emmet Prendergast's ma, Dylan Murphy's ma who's deaf, Sonya Gosling's ma. And a load of other mas who I didn't know. There were about 24 different mas in total. I think I felt guilty watching them, but it was a new type of guilt. Not like a guilt because I'd told a lie, or because I'd taken one of Jerry's Mars Bars from the cupboard beside his bed. It was like a dirty guilt that I had to keep secret. Like when Art Ó Laoire called me a fridget in front of Nessa. At first, the videos of all the mas made me kind of excited – it was sex, like on the German tapes – but then, when I really had a think about it, I started to not like the ma tape, because I couldn't tell if the women really wanted to be taped or not, or if they wanted me to look at it. I thought about being big enough to box the head off Fintan Ó Laoire. Sonya Gosling's ma is so nice to me. Last year, when I climbed over Larkin's wall to get my ball, Mr Larkin said he'd ring the guards and I'd go to jail. I was terrified. It was Mrs Gosling who saw me crying. She told me that the guards would never arrest me for climbing over walls, and I didn't feel frightened anymore. And now I'd seen her like this, but she didn't know I'd seen her like this, so how could I talk to her again in a normal way? I didn't know the name of what I was feeling and I missed being angry about ice creams with frozen chocolate on them.

I got up off the couch and opened a box of Fintan's muesli and ate it dry with my hands. Pacing around the lino floor in dim light, feeling red and boily, feeling soiled. Below the mantelpiece were these two big ornamental elephant tusks. I think they were real because beside it was a photograph of Fintan looking younger, in like, safari gear, with his arm around a black fella who was smiling, and Fintan had a rifle strapped around himself. Normally, I'd think the gun was cool looking, and I'd want to call to Art's house back home and ask if his da takes him shooting, and if I could go with them the next time. But I didn't. Because in that moment, I realised that Fintan was treating the mas like they were game, he was hunting them. But he couldn't turn the mas into ivory and hang them off a mantelpiece, so he put them on tape instead.

All my wanking in Trabolgan felt different now. When Paul told me the stories about the hooers in Barcelona, it sounded like a big adventure. He made it funny and I'd want to run away to wank about it. To imagine myself in his position. My wanking felt wrong, so I made a deal with myself that I'd only do it from now on if I absolutely had to. I wouldn't do it loads of times in a day. I'd convinced myself that wanking feels good because it's like sweets or ice cream. If you have too much you'll get sick.

Bad things will happen. Like seeing everyone's mas having sex and not being able to talk to them again.

I switched the TV over from the video. I wanted to watch *Saved by the Bell* or *Fresh Prince* to take my mind off the mas. Instead, I landed on Sky News. The newsreader had this look on her face. Her voice had a high-pitched trepid warble and her eyes were kind of open an awful lot, a bit extra like, no blinking out of her. Two planes had crashed into a skyscraper over in New York, and the people who were talking about it looked really shook. Usually, no matter how scary the news is, the people reading it out are calm, and when you see that then you know everything is OK. Like on an aeroplane when it's bumpy so you look at the air hostess's face, and if she's calm then everything is OK. This was different. A man was falling from the building, he looked like a dot and I started to think about ma and da in Israel and about the dream where they were on fire. My heart thumped in my throat, and my face was vibrating. I began to believe that all of this was happening because of my wanking. Because I'd listened to Paul's stories, and because I'd broken into all the houses, and because I saw the tapes with the mas. Those planes crashed because of what I'd been doing. It was my punishment for being so filthy and horrible and not knowing when to stop.

In that moment, the only way I could figure out how to stop this, how to stop more planes crashing into buildings, was to make it right. I needed to stop Fintan Ó Laoire from recording more mas. So I hurried towards the wardrobe where he kept all the tapes. At the top, there were shoeboxes and a big carry case with his camera. It was the type that taped directly onto VHS so the recordings didn't need to be sent to the chemist to be developed. I set the camera up and pointed it at the couch.

I was ready to tape over the tape with all the mas. Tape over it with me talking directly to Fintan, telling him that I know what he's doing and that he has to stop, because I'll tell everyone. And that if he doesn't stop recording mas and I don't stop wanking, then awful things will happen on the news.

But before I could, Granda Jerry climbed in the window. He was in a purple dressing gown and his face was silver with that long stubble. He had a Tesco lager in his hand and another hung from his dressing-gown pocket.

'Did you see the news? Did you see the news? It's like the *Giants of the Galtee Mountains*,' he shouted. I told him I did and I asked how he knew I was here.

'Paul told me you wank in all the houses so I checked every house and this was the only one left.'

I froze. Every bit of anger and fear in me, every bit of guilt came out, and I started shouting so loudly that my head hurt and I felt like getting sick.

'Shut up, shut up, shut up.'

Jerry was too drunk to take notice of how upset I was and just said, 'There's great energy in those screams, there's an actor in you.' The door of the chalet opened. It was Paul.

'What the fuck is all the noise, lads?' He pointed at me with a stubby finger. 'You. This was the one fucking place I told you not to come to, lad. This is a private gaff, we can't be in here. I had to go up to head office to get the key.'

Jerry was stumbling around over by the couch and had found the video camera. He pulled a violet throw from an armchair and lobbed it at Paul.

'You, put that over your fucking head there. You're going to be the Warlock of Glisheen.'

'Get out of the fucking gaff, I'm serious, ye're trespassing,' retorted Paul.

'I'll make sure your wife finds out about every story you told me of Barcelona, lad. Put on that over your head and be the Warlock of Glisheen. Fuck is wrong with you telling that stuff to this young lad?'

Hearing that Paul had told Jerry the Barcelona stories made me feel slightly better. It felt like less of a secret, and for the first time, I had a sense that Jerry was actually looking out for me. That he'd been watching from a distance all along. He had a manic look to him now, a type of energy that cut through his drunkenness. He ripped the stuffing out of a pillow and bit two eyeholes in the cover. He dragged over a pouffe and ushered me to stand on it. I did.

'You'll be one of the giants of the Galtee Mountains, lad.'

I placed the cushion cover mask over my head. Jerry removed his dressing gown, and was down to his Y-front jocks. He pressed record on the tape player. For the next twenty minutes, in Fintan Ó Laoire's Trabolgan chalet, we performed *The Giants of the Galtee Mountains*. Jerry just roared Paul's lines at him, and he said them out of fear. The great hero in the *Giants of the Galtee Mountains* is a postman called Bart the Brontannas. He is the only person who can speak to the giants. He does this by consuming human hair that he steals from barber shops, or eats directly off the heads of people who are asleep. In act two, there is a battle between Bart the Brontannas, played by Jerry, and the Warlock of Glisheen, played by Paul. Bart wins the battle by eating the warlock's hair, and Jerry really did it. He stood on Paul's chest and took a bite out of his fringe. Paul screamed. After this, it was my role as a giant of the Galtee Mountains to inform Bart that

JFK would be assassinated in a year's time. And that the only way to stop it would be for Bart to turn the light switch in his bathroom on and off seventy-four times each hour until 1988, when JFK dies of natural causes. I knew all my lines off by heart. For the first time, I enjoyed Jerry's play, because I knew it was taping over Fintan Ó Laoire's footage of all the mas, and this meant that no more bad things would happen on the news. When the third act was done, Paul left. He didn't say goodbye to me or to Jerry. I watched him walk back up the road towards his prefab. It was raining, and he didn't even try to run or cover his head. He just walked, getting wet, as if there were no rain at all.

I took the cushion cover off my head. Performing *The Giants of the Galtee Mountains* had sobered Jerry up. He had a new look on his face. Like he'd just confessed a massive sin or been given an extra ten years to live. This great mood of relief came over him. I didn't tell him that he'd taped over the footage of everyone's mothers having sex with Fintan Ó Laoire. He didn't need to know. That had to be a secret that only I knew and Fintan knew. Jerry looked at me, and his eyes weren't jittery or moving around the room like they usually do. He was staring me straight in the eyes and he said, 'It's out of my system, young lad. It's out now, I have it recorded. It lives on the tape player now. It's not in my head anymore. I'm free of *The Giants of the Galtee Mountains*. I can stop. I can stop.'

'Paul was great as the Warlock of Glisheen,' I said.

'He was. All along, I thought it was a stage play. It wasn't, it was a television drama. That's what it was. And now we have it,' Jerry whispered to me, but really to himself. He took the VHS tape out of the recorder and put it in his dressing-gown pocket beside the Tesco lager.

We left Trabolgan three days later. I spent the last days not wanking, and doing everything I could to not think about wanking. Any time I thought about anything sexy, like Nessa's thighs, or Paul's stories, or the German porn, I would just turn the light switch in the bathroom on and off seventy-four times like in Jerry's play. This made me not want to wank. Before we made it back home to Douglas, Jerry stopped off in an audio visual shop where they make copies of tapes. They made fifty copies in under an hour and we arrived home with a box of them in the boot.

'If I sit down now and watch the tape we made, I'll only be critical of it. I'll find something wrong with the performance and I won't show it to a soul. I'll be stuck with the play in my head again. So I need to do this. I need to put it out there as a finished work and let people see it. Only then will I give myself the satisfaction of watching it.'

That night we wrote 'The Giants of the Galtee Mountains' on the tapes, and Jerry put one in the letterbox of every house in our estate.

I went to bed. As I lay there, I started to get horny thoughts again. I was thinking about Paul's stories. I couldn't stop it. I gave in and started wanking. I broke my promise to myself. I was interrupted by Jerry's shouting from downstairs in the living room.

'What the fuck is this? This isn't *The Giants of the Galtee Mountains*. Is that Martina Goff?'

My wanking had caused this. I could have prevented it with the light switch. Someone else might say to me, 'Don't be ridiculous. Jerry just didn't press record. He's old, how would he know how to use a video camera?' But I knew it was because of my wanking. When I wank, bad things happen.

THE HELLFIRE SCUM

n a darkened flat overlooking Centra.

— I'm a big fan of death because it's the only certainty we have, and the human condition can be summed up as a perpetual struggle for certainty. We don't cope too well with uncertainty, do we? Think about it – what causes you most of your stress in your daily existence? Chances are it's not shit that's happening now, but not being sure of what's happening next. Am I right? That tends to be our present condition of unease. If we could tolerate uncertainty there'd be no need for religion. What's religion only a set of rules that defines certainty? That's what priests, rabbis and imams get paid to do. They roar and shout about owning books that are balls deep in certainty. The gospel truth. When presented with the only true certainty – death – it's so challenging to them that they then have to preach the ambiguous uncertainty of the afterlife. Throw certain and definite cessation of all existence into religion and it shits its pants and gets dragged out of the nightclub by bouncers.

Shower of messers, boy. Here's a certainty … You and everyone you love are going to die, every dog you've ever seen, every person you've watched on TV or exercising in an Argos catalogue, every tree you've climbed, every person you've read about on the door of a toilet in a petrol station, they are all going to die. The sun is going to die – it's technically middle-aged – that's a certainty. That's pure depressing. But if you stick with the thought, and don't flutter away from it or go out and buy a new pair of denims, as we tend to do, it can be fair empowering, because you can use that certainty of inevitable cessation to appreciate that you're alive right now and you have full control – not full control over what happens to you, but full control over your attitude towards what happens. And you can use the certainty that everyone you know is going to die to cop on to yourself if you're treating them like gowls. And that's a fucking liberating and delicious sandwich to stick your teeth into. It's not the delectable garlic-and-cheese chip of religion and heaven, but it's a humble slice of brown bread that will keep you ticking away at a steady pace. Do you hear me, Dúsaillaigh?

—Dan, I'm not too sure how to say this in a way … in a way that's not insensitive to you, but … did you bring me here to tell me that you're thinking of ending your life?

—Hahaha, ah Jaysus, Dúsaillaigh, no no no no. You'll have another slice of Battenberg, you will?

—Oh, I will.

—The marzipan is great, the way it'll creep up on you. Isn't it smashing altogether? Like, you get the hit of sweetness on the palate, and you're thinking, what the fuck is this at all? Is it liquorice I'm tasting?

—Indeed, but the two-colour sponge, Dan?

—The fucking two-colour sponge, Dús. You have it in one. That's the joy of Battenberg. The sponge takes the brute force out of the marzipan, and it allows the bouquet to open up into the nostrils.

—It does, and what taste is that, Dan? The marzipan, like. Is it just a marzipan taste? Is it its own taste, like Coca-Cola?

—Well, I'll tell you now. And here's the interesting thing about the olfactory experience of consuming marzipan.

—Any chance of tea? Turn on a light, you will?

—Kettle's boiling away over on the stove. Bear with me a small bit, now, while I tell you this. And don't be afraid to put butter on Battenberg either, makes it very lively – there'll be a fine lump of Kerrygold there on that red dish. Got that dish in Portugal. Lad in a wheelchair makes them, handmade job, has his own kiln. But come here to me, Dúsaillaigh, here's the thing about the olfactory experience of consuming marzipan.

—Go on.

—If you were to ever … get that taste, the marzipan taste, in your mouth under any other circumstance or situation than consuming marzipan, it wouldn't be a great sign at all.

—I'll pour in my own milk, Dan, 'tis grand, just a splash in the cup – I like it weak. What do you mean by that, that it wouldn't be a great sign?

—Well, the taste of marzipan is actually almonds.

—Ah, go'way, it is and all. Fucking almonds. How am I only realising that now?

—There you are, it's almonds. And the interesting thing is, if I was to hand you an almond now, it wouldn't taste like marzipan. Marzipan has the taste of what you've been told an almond tastes like.

—That's the head blown off me now for the day, Dan. You were always some man for the knowledge.

—But c'mere to me, Dús, like I was saying, if you ever got that specific taste outside of the practice of eating marzipan, you'd be in awful trouble.

—Yes, that bit, go on, tell me.

—Well, it'd mean one of two things. You'd either be ready to have a fit, which might be an indication of a brain tumour, or you'd be up to your oxters in muck in a trench in the French theatre of World War I.

—I'm lost.

—There's a chemical by the name of hydrogen cyanide – deadly poison, now. It makes your chest fill up with fluid, and you drown in your own lungs.

—Holy Jaysus!

—Yes, nasty stuff. And hydrogen cyanide has the smell of almonds. Well, not almonds – the marzipan smell.

—Almond memory.

—That's the one.

—And what about the brain tumour, Dan?

—I don't know the answer to that, but I was watching a fella on a HBO thing. It wasn't *The Sopranos*, another thing.

—Tony is some bowzy. Was it *Breaking Bad*?

—He is, but there was another thing I was watching – *Breaking Bad* isn't HBO either – but I was watching a thing, and your man got a fit from a brain tumour, and I remember him saying that he could taste almonds before it hit him, so that's where I heard that one. You'll have another slice?

—Go on, sure. Tell me this anyway, Dan, what type of clothes is it you're wearing? Very strange. Turn on a light and show me?

—I'll get to that in a minute.

—Is it a type of tracksuit? Is that why you've me here, because I haven't the first clue why you're after calling me here at all?

—Well, it wasn't just for the Battenberg sponge, Dús.

—Hahahaha. I wasn't thinking that was the reason, now, to be fair.

—No. I'll tell you about my clothes now in a while. Just chat with me a bit first, because it's been a long time. And I miss the sound of your voice, you ould prick. When was the last time we sat down together – '98, '99, I'd say? It must have been at the Drip's thirty-first.

— Hahaha. That was a hairy weekend. And the Drip had the two wans from Kinnegad in the tent with him.

—Jaysus, Dús, and he was turning on the torch inside coz he thought we'd see the silhouettes of their hoops, fucking Ace Ventura.

—Hahahaha. We'd a fine group of lunatics when you think back, hadn't we?

—We did, and then we went off on our own ways, sure.

—What's the Drip up to now, Dan? Is he still into Megadeth?

It is getting darker outside. The flat smells like winter chimneys and Battenberg. The air becomes colder through the single glazing.

—He's in Vancouver, selling African grey parrots, trains them to talk and all. They'd go for the arse end of three grand if you'd a chatty one.

—And is he settled?

—No, he's one of those involuntary celibates by the go of his Facebook. I think there might be a strain of a Nazi in him, to tell you the truth.

—Would you trust him not to be a Nazi around the parrots?

—His clients are looking for it. He trains the parrots to say all sorts of shite, and the clients make money putting the parrots on the internet.

—They'd put it up on Wavin Pipe?

—YouTube.

—I know 'tis YouTube, you eejit, I'm joshing. And would you say the parrots have an idea of what they're saying? If they're from Africa, like?

—You know, that's an interesting one now, and it's mad that we were only talking about almonds because, you know, a parrot's brain is only about the size of an almond.

—Same as the Drip's then.

—HAHAHAHAHAHAHAHA!

—Are you still backpatching, Dan?

—I'm not, Dús. I've a Triumph in the shed, and I'll give her road maybe once a month, but I haven't the gumption for anything organised.

—Sure, I'd to sell my own. We put it towards the cost of Avril's nursing degree. Ah, they were fucking great times though, weren't they? Looking back like. Remember Goony had the Harley with the big seat and the wide handlebars that he brought down from Dublin?

—Ah, she was a great hog, you'd hear her below in Ballinspittle. Poor ould Goony.

—The poor fella.

—I gave up the backpatching not long after you. The rest of the lads took up with the Devil's Buthers.

—Ah, but you couldn't bate the Hellfire Scum, though. We were something else. Do you remember the meet in Kilkee – '97, I'd say it was? Do you remember we caught the Bandidos lad from Galway, and Guff made him ate the rooster's end of a hurl? And we fucked off into a load of Linden Village two litres down by the pollock holes, Sepultura blaring, 'Roots Bloody Roots', and the crowd who had the guitar player, Dimebag, fucking Pantera, man.

—I fucking remember it well, Dúsaillaigh, will you go'way.

—Tin of red Dax for the ponytails. I'd say the Drip has a skullet at this stage. He must be fifty now, is he? Is he ever back at home at all?

—And the fucking hash, Dús?

—'RA hash. The squidgy Libyan stuff.

—Smell of black pudding when it hit the flame.

—Sure, the Good Friday Agreement ruined all that.

—The stuff that's around now isn't too bad, White Widow, Blue Cheese. You'd be stuck to the couch, though.

—I couldn't touch it now. Claire is seventeen, she'd know what it is.

—Fuck off, is Claire seventeen?

—She is, Dan, growing a fine arse like her ma's too.

—Hahaha, you sick cunt, you're still a fucking sick cunt.

—Ah sure, look, you can't even make a joke nowadays or the feminists would have your balls.

—And how's Avril, Dús?

—She's a nurse below in Cork University Hospital, not a drop in fifteen years.

—Fair play to her, and how is she nursing with the big tattoo of the blood eagle on her shoulders?

—Whisht.

—Hahahahahaha.

—Hahahahahahahaha.

The room glows a bright orange. Dúsailligh notices there is a powerful streetlight directly outside Dan's window. This makes Dús frown and his lips purse and he produces a nervous sucking noise. He becomes more aware of the bang of chimneys hanging in the damp. He stares at the Battenberg and the red Portuguese butter dish.

—There's another two slices in that Battenberg, sure. You'll have one more?

—Of course, it's fucking unreal. I'm nearly thinking of buying one on the way home.

—The backpatching got dark, though, Dús, when the Butchers got stuck in. They're the real deal. They're bigger than Kinsale, bigger than Cork. Into all sorts of muck.

—Sure don't I know, ould speed and heroin.

—No, the parrots.

—Parrots?

—The parrots. The Butchers go down to South Africa, and they come back with rhino horns and wild-parrot eggs for the racists.

—It's the new golden triangle?

—It'd be more of a golden rectangle.

—Didn't you say they're going to South Africa and coming back with parrot eggs and rhino horns, Dan? Wouldn't that just be a line? Not a shape?

—They are, but it would need a third stop to make it a triangle. They'd have to stop in Amsterdam or somewhere and then come back to Kinsale. You'd have your triangle then.

—So they're just going directly to South Africa and coming back to Kinsale?

—That's the one. And they bring back parrot eggs in the tanks of the bikes. Frozen in nitrogen. *Jurassic Park* style.

—That's not any class of shape, Dan. So that's how the Drip ended up over in Vancouver? Which came first – Vancouver or the parrots?

—The parrots. Ah, they're only making an eejit out of the poor ould Drip, away on YouTube, and he has a Canadian accent on him and the hairstyle still like Dave Mustaine, and you'd see him pretending to be hatching the eggs under his jacket and telling the eggs about Rudolf Hess. Talking into his armpits, like. The racists love it. He'd be getting ten thousand views, like. The Butchers are pulling all those strings.

—Nasty fuckers so?

—Machiavellian … C'mere, are you still into whiskey? I've a drop in the wardrobe that I want to bring in to you.

—Ah, I can't, Dan, the shuckas have breathalysers after every roundabout now as soon as we hit the wrong side of November.

—Dús, I'll have to force it into you, just a taste, and I'll tell you why now as soon as I bring it out.

—Only a nose so, Dan, no more. I'm serious.

—Here, now, tiny swig of that, and if you look at the name on the bottle I'll kill you. You've to guess.

—Jaysus, that's powerful. It's a Bushmills, is it?

—It's not. How much would you say?

—Between thirty-five and forty euro.

—Eighteen euro I paid for that.

—Fuck off, did you pay eighteen euro for that stuff? It's a potion.

—I did ... Aldi.

—Aldi?

—Aldi.

—I'll have to pick that up, 'Highland Black'. Avril is in Aldi non-stop. Hold on and I get a photo of the bottle. Put it down alongside the butter. Turn on a light there.

—Not yet, use the flash. Is that the new iPhone?

—The X, it's a beast, Dan. Wait till you see the quality of this picture in a minute.

—I suppose the phone comes with the job, does it? How long are you with Apple now? Gogsy told me you're a supervisor?

—How's Gogsy getting on? I'm team leader, Dan, nearly eight years. Fucking great place, now, in fairness. Held me down during the recession, to tell you the truth.

—Sure, don't I know. I was above in Raychem in Limerick. Nothing here, man. Dole or fuck off.

—I didn't want to be rude, Dan, but with no disrespect, how are you doing? You've a grand flat here, like, but the cold is pure fierce, and by the go of the black mould above that window, I doubt you've the heat on much at all, have you?

—That's part of the reason I asked you down here, Dús.

—Dan, ta fuck, I love the neck of you, we're fucking Hellfire Scum to the end, boy, we're brothers. But I can't be giving you money. Claire has the leaving coming up – she's looking at DIT next year. Avril's earning nothing the way they have the nurses either. I appreciate the Battenberg but –

—Ah no, Dús, do you honestly think I'd drag you back to Kinsale after all these years to ask for a loan of money?

—It's not that I wouldn't give it to you if I had it.

—Relax, man, I know well you're a good skin, will you stop. If I get very bad, my ma gives me a few quid for the gas. I'm grand.

—Then why have you me down here?

—I was watching a film about Steve Jobs on the tablet.

—Ashton Kutcher?

—That's the one. And I was, just, enamoured – enamoured is the only word for it – by his vision, and his tenacity, and the innovation fucking falling off him, like. And then I'd heard from Gogsy that you were above in Cork, supervising in Apple, and I thought you might have an in.

—A job? You're looking for a job with us? Dan, I could put in a word, like, to Gerry – he's up in recruitment. But that's all HR stuff. You'd have to email in a CV, and it could be some prick over in San Francisco who opens it. They've this all sewn up, like. I wouldn't have any swing on that. You can't just walk in and start inside in Apple on a Monday, like.

—It's not a job I'm looking for. It's a bit more ambitious than that.

—You're a gas ticket. What in the fuck are you looking for so? Jaysus, that drop of the Aldi stuff was enough to make me want another. Do you remember Salthill, '95? Your one who looked like Rod Stewart got the lickout on the snooker table off Shirty Hartigan? And Pluck faked a fit in front of the bar manager? Brained the cunt who spat on his backpatch? Do you remember that?

—Have you heard of Cameron Downes?

—Have I fuck. He's visiting us in two weeks. I'm drafting the presentation.

—Ya, but do you know what Cameron Downes did over in Japan?

—I don't know about Japan, but he's head of innovation with ourselves. I heard he was out in Silicon Valley when he was a young fella.

—He's the man responsible for mobile phones, like.

—Ah now, Dan, slow down.

—Dús, what's the reason Cameron Downes is coming to visit ye in Apple in Cork in two weeks? Tell me the reason.

—He's getting us ready for 5G.

—Exactly. And how would you react if I told you he was the man responsible for inventing 1G?

—I'd say fair play?

—He was a junior developer in Nippon, Dús. They rolled out the first 1G network ever in Japan in the late seventies. He came up with 1G. That's the start of mobile phones.

—What in the love of Christ are you getting at? Have you brought me to Kinsale to give me tips for my presentation? I'm fierce confused here.

Dan is excited as he moves towards the kitchenette. He turns on the main light in the room. It is a 300-watt fluorescent strip. The room illuminates in a clean blue white. The tarnishes on the walls are exposed in their honesty. The faded mauve carpet is unwell and is littered with receipts and coins and has archipelagos of squashed chewing gum, gone black from the soles of boots. The light makes the room feel more cold than it is. Dúsaillaigh is worried. The orange street lamp outside is no longer visible through the window due to the blue fluorescent glare. Dan extends his arms out like an angel's wings.

—I need you to put me in a room with Cameron Downes, Dús, before you give that presentation.

—Is there a video camera hidden in here or something? Is the Drip in on this? What the fuck are you wearing? I fucking knew earlier this had something to do with the quare outfit you have on. Jaysus, that's odd-looking in the light now. Is it a suit or a tracksuit? It's not a jumpsuit, is it?

—I'm wearing the future of your company.

—You look like an ould lad whose chin fell off in a bookies.

—I'm gonna have to ask you to take this seriously, Dús, because I've an invention that Steve Jobs would hop out of the grave for, and I'm offering you first dibs.

—Are you gone stone mad, Dan?

—I'm not.

—Am I after getting dragged to Kinsale because you've an invention that you want me to show to Cameron Downes? Are you for real? Is that what this is about?

—It is.

—Out with it then.

—You're looking at it.

Under the full blue lumen of the fluorescent bulb, Dan outstretches his left leg, then his right, finally turning slowly to reveal his back.

—So the fucking tracksuit you're wearing is the invention? Apple isn't selling clothes, brother. Are you sure you're not under stress, Dan?

—I couldn't be feeling any better, Dús. It's not a tracksuit, sure – let me explain a bit. Have a feel of the hem first. Do you feel that?

—There's a feel of fire-retardant carpet off it.

—It's custom tweed, man. This is only the prototype. I need an investor for the final garment. This cost me fifteen hundred euro for the fabric alone.

—Dan, I need to start thinking about road here … Howld on, so you stitched it all together yourself?

—I did.

—And what's the story with the arse?

—I'd to eyeball the whole thing, couldn't get the arse right. There's a few things wrong with it. Take a squint at this leg here when I walk.

—Ah ya, it rises a bit.

—You have it now, the left leg rises up. Watch, if I take a step here with the right, you see that? It goes up a bit on the opposite leg.

—You couldn't be walking around like that. You'd need to take it in around the arse or the balls even.

—Ya, there's a few things that are off with its architecture. It's not about the design, though, Dús. This is wearable technology.

—Where'd you learn to stitch a suit?

—YouTube tutorials, sure. It's not about the style of it, though.

—And they've tutorials on YouTube for making wearable technology?

—They do, Dús, but that's not the important bit. It's about the fabric itself. The tweed is the technology.

—Tweed's not technology.

—About two years ago, I picked up an ould tweed jacket inside in the charity shop down there by Mount Street. It was after my thirty-fifth.

—Tough year.

—Ya, so it was after my thirty-fifth, and I wanted to chance a more mature look. The waistcoat and backpatch wasn't working anymore, the belly was sticking out. It wasn't right for a man in his mid-thirties.

—Don't I fucking know it, Dan.

—I was getting worried that I was looking like there's a pity on me, truth be told. So I flaked on this tweed jacket, probably belonged to an ould lad, but I wore her anyway with the leather Stetson on my head, and I still had the boots too.

—Like an ironic kind of thing?

—An ironic thing, Dús, ya, so there was still a bit of the rocker vibe, but with a maturity about the torso. So after a few weeks of wearing it, I chanced it bare-chest, like.

—Mad bastard.

—Ya, it was July now. So I went down to Houlihan's for a cone with a Flake, and I had the tweed on with full bare skin, and it was itchy as fuck, very bad now, making my skin red.

—Fuck that.

—But I was loving it.

—You were loving it?

—I was. It was enamouring, like – enamouring is the only word for it – the itch. There was an orgasmic tickle to it.

—Dirty fucker.

—So I decided to get a pair of tweed pants.

—Go on.

—And before long, I was head to toe in tweed. And every inch of my body was awakened, invigorated, with this non-stop itch. Not the annoying kind; this lively itch, like a chip that just had salt poured on it. It brought out the vigour in me.

—But how is that technology, Dan?

—Here's the thing. So at this stage, I'd become addicted to the feeling. I was panging for it, like. I had to start wearing it in bed and all. I couldn't bear a moment's existence if I was living it in a soft fabric. Even the sound of sandpaper, or a match scraping off the side of a matchbox, it would make me salivate, like.

—Was it sexual, a kink, like?

—Nothing like that. I'd nearly refer to it as spiritual. It was a type of asceticism. It keeps you out of your head, grounds you in the present moment.

—Buddhist craic?

—More of a St Brendan vibe. So that's when I made bigger plans. To find a more abrasive tweed. But there was fuck all available. I even went up as far as Donegal, to a wool mill, and they had nothing with the right shag to it. I needed something more industrial. So I got in contact with Fecky Nevin below in Killarney.

—Fecky fucking Nevin? From the Dirt Angels? There's a name that brings back memories, now. Do you remember him over in Newcastle? We'd to call off a sesh after he found the lump in his testicle?

—The same Fecky, that's him.

—How the fuck is Fecky?

—He's minding a load of goats.

—How'd he get stuck into goats?

—The uncle.

—Jaysus.

—So I went after Fecky for goat's wool.

—Goats have wool?

—It'd be more of a wire, now, especially Killarney goats, they've years of wire bred into them due to the north wind they get below. But I told Fecky, anyway, about my issue with the tweed, and he gave me the bones of a tonne of goat wire.

—And how'd you get on with it?

—I brought it up to Donegal in a Dyna, Dús, and had it spun into a tweed the likes of which the world has never seen, in terms of its abrasion, like.

—And is that what you have on now?

—'Tis, this is full Killarney goat's tweed. But there's a quareness to the consistency of this suit that you won't find with other fabrics.

—Is it doing it for you? The itch?

—You've no idea. But there's more. Take a look at that.

—It's a digital watch.

—Look at the reading on the screen, Dús.

—It's gibberish.

—You try it on.

—8.36 p.m.

—Now give it back to me.

—It's gibberish again. What the fuck?

—So when I started wearing this particular suit, Dús, all I expected was that it would satiate my desire for the itch. I'd developed a tolerance, like, and was getting withdrawals. So I needed the goat's wire tweed, something more powerful, more bang for the buck.

—I have you.

—But mad shit started happening.

—Like what?

—I'd step outside for a smoke, and by the time I'd have gone back inside, three months could have passed. Before I'd have gotten my head around that even happening, I'd be back where I was before I went out for the smoke in the first place. Now I know what you're fucking thinking.

—What was inside in that smoke is what I'm thinking. The lemony haze or whatever you called it.

—No, regular fags, John Player, no weed. Swear to fuck. And it started to get worse the more I moved around, like, the longer I walked.

—How'd you mean?

—One day I walked up as far as Cremins' bóithrín, a good stretch, like. And there were women walking past me in rags, then other fellas on horses with, like, military uniforms, but years-old uniforms, now, red-coat jobs. And their faces went white when they saw me, and I went white when I saw them. Other times then, now I fucking swear, I saw dinosaurs, big fuckers, man.

—Dan, are you taking the piss again?

—I'm not. I saw, like, a Tyrannosaurus up above by the gannet hill, and he was chasing what looked like a Jesuit, but covered in sparkly jewels. And I'd look away and look back, and the Tyrannosaurus was wearing clothes.

—What type?

—Like flares, flared-type slacks, up as far as his thighs. Then I'd run, out of terror, and the landscape would turn hot, with volcanoes, and I'd be struggling to breathe until I'd slow down. And when I got really slow, it'd be freezing, and there'd be a load of cold metal huts, like fridges, dotted all over Kinsale, with these creatures who had arses for faces and they were small, maybe two-foot tall, and they could talk with their minds, not moving their mouths, and I could understand them, told me that we should start eating copper instead of food if we're to save the planet.

—This is a fucking stretch, Dan.

—Are you going to do away with that last slice of the Battenberg or will I?

—No, this is a bit too much. I think I'm done with the Battenberg.

—You sure now?

—Leave it there for a bit. I'm uncertain.

A silence commands the space, with the danger of an awkwardness.

—How's all this sitting with you, Dús?

—So is it some style of hallucination that comes over you when you're wearing the tweed suit?

—It's as real as day – it's no hallucination.

—So what's your read on it then, Dan? Is it a midlife crisis, do you think?

—I've never heard of a midlife crisis expressing itself like that, now, Dús.

—What about Bovril Teeling? He tried to grow spaniels in a test tube.

—He'd a bit of a want in him, though, always did. This here is fucking real. You know the way the best blades are diamond-tipped? Like, if they were cutting into steel, they'd use a diamond to do it because it's harder?

—Well, it's density.

—Same thing.

—Not necessarily, Dan.

—I think I've stumbled upon a discovery that'd change the very nature of reality as we know it. I think this goat's wire tweed is the diamond of the fabric world.

—The diamond of the fabric world?

—The diamond of the fabric world. This tweed is so abrasive that when I shuffle about in it, it causes little rips in the fabric of time. And the more aggressively I move, the more it cuts into hours and fortnights and years, and that's what I've been experiencing. It's why the watch doesn't work on my wrist.

—Howld on, the suit is allowing you to time travel?

—That's a simplistic way of putting it, Dúsaillaigh. I'm not going forward or backward in time when I put on the tweed. To be honest, that's more of an illusion that's been sold to us by watchmakers. This linear time business, it's a huge lie. It's just our ould feeble heads trying to know the unknowable. My experience is more like I'm merging with it through the rips. The suit allows me to become past, present, future, beginning, end, all at once. I'm everything that ever was, and everything that wasn't, and everything that hasn't yet.

—Can I have a go of the suit, then?

—No.

—How do I know you're telling the truth? You could have just fucked a magnet under your watch and that's what makes it go banjaxed on your wrist.

—The tweed technology isn't tested properly at all. You've to remember, I spent nearly two years being fully dependent on the tweed to itch my skin. I built up a tolerance. If you were to try on so much as a waistcoat made out of this, Dús, you'd be torn to shreds, like a cheese grater.

—Fuck me.

—Ya, not to mention what it would do to your existence. You could get lost. You'd be stuck in an hour forever, like – you'd never escape it. I tried it with the Learys' cat, made goat's wire galoshes for him – he went sideways.

—Is he alive?

—If you could call it living.

—What would you call it?

—He's at the back of Maxol, buried in a box that's the shape of a year. Enslaved in a condition that can only be described as a soup of his birth and death.

—And, supposing then, Dan, that this is real, and you're not having a fucking laugh out of me. How has no one else discovered this? About tweed, like?

—That's the thing, Dús, we *have* discovered it. It's been staring us in the face all along. I'm just the first to put a name to it. What about Christ?

—What about Christ?

—You need to take a look at the manger where he was born. When young Mary birthed him, I'd wager that he was wrapped in a goat's wire shawl. And as the infant Christ started moving his legs, or doing whatever it is newborns do, the shawl would have been itching away at the fabric of time. Making small rips. That's how he managed to be both his own da and his own son all at once. That's the mystery of the Holy Trinity right there. But it's no mystery no more. And I'd confidently wager that the teenage Christ might have kept a piece of the shawl with him at all times and turned water into wine, and cured the blind, and did all sorts.

—This could be fucking big, Dan. But I still have this part of me that thinks you're gone stone mad.

—You've to trust me. Think of everything we've been through. How many times have I taken a box in the face for you? How many times have I been there to throw boxes for you, and you the same for me? Who brought you Lucozade and porn mags when you fell off the bike in Belfast and nearly lost your shins? You were an invalid convalescent for the donkey's end of six months. The fucking casts up to your thighs and Avril wiping your arse and pulling you off and I feeding you mashed parsnips through a rolled-up newspaper? We go back, brother. We're Hellfire Scum, man. This is why I need you to get me into Apple to speak to Cameron Downes. I'm coming to you as a brother of the Scum of Hell. Nothing more, nothing less. Anyway, think of the applications of this tweed to someone like Apple, or Google if you won't take me up.

—But, Dan, like I said, I can't see them branching out into fashion.

—No, I want the tweed in phones, in laptops, full 5G compliant.

—Now that's different. Go on.

—How long does Claire spend on her iPhone?

—She's stuck into it all day.

—And she's using social media, is she not? Instagram, Twitter, whatever.

—She is.

—If the past ten years have taught us anything, Dús, it's that we can use social media to edit how people see us. We can change our faces, alter our words, make ourselves appear more successful than we are. What if our phones actually let us do this with real life?

—A tweed phone?

—A phone that uses the abrasive qualities of goat's wire tweed to hack time. To let each of us pause, or go back to last night and unsay that thing we said, or drink less. Or go forward two weeks and prepare the right words for an argument.

—We'd be selling certainty.

—Yes, we'd be selling fucking certainty.

—But, like, how could everyone be fucking around with time? Wouldn't that be madness?

—We're doing it already, we just don't control it. Every single possibility of every action has its own universe for that possibility. So if you choose to not have that last slice of Battenberg, there's another version of you off in another plane of reality that chooses to eat the Battenberg. Every choice has its own little universe that pops up like bubbles rising in a pint. Infinite possibilities. Time is unique to all of us – we carry it around like a shell on our backs.

—This is interesting, Dan, I'm not going to lie.

—Are you going to do away with that last slice of the Battenberg or will I?

—Go on sure, I'll have it.

—Take the last of the butter there too.

—No, fuck it, we'll go halves on it.

—Lovely, the last piece. Sharing it. Like true Scum brothers. And hopefully we'll be eating this as a type of celebration, ya?

—How long would it take you to tell all this to Cameron Downes?

—Ten minutes max.

—This didn't take ten minutes, Dan.

—That was due to the Battenberg.

—If he doesn't take to the idea, Dan, I'm gone, like, job terminated. This would go against everything in my Apple contract. I shouldn't even be talking to him myself, let alone bringing you onto the premises. I'd have to sneak you in.

—I'll arrive in the suit. I'll tell him everything I just told you. We're Hellfire Scum, Dús. We're brothers. We'll be a team, like it's '96 again. This will make us fucking rich.

—Hellfire Scum.

—Hellfire Scum.

—Crack open that Lidl stuff again, just a drop.

—The Aldi stuff?

—That's the one, ya.

INRI

MAURA

You need to relax. Your life is drifting sideways, and you feel nothing you do has any meaning. 'Twenty-eight is a proper grown-up age' are the words on the text you send to Brenda. The Twitter likes don't fill the hole anymore. You no longer experience affirmation from other people being jealous of you. This is starting to seem silly and pointless. The music that the twenty-year-olds like sounds like bad music to you, but you won't let anyone hear you say that, not yet.

You've started to stay up later and later – not in a planned way, it would just happen. You'd make hot milk with turmeric and cinnamon. You'd have your sheets clean and fresh – you'd spray them with a homemade rose-scented infusion you bought from a Korean woman on Etsy. You added her on Instagram after and you call her your friend. Your room is tidy, it is clean. Egyptian sheets are so crisp. Under them, your legs release all of that achy tension. Your calves celebrate the sheer magnificence of that cotton on skin. You move your arms and legs outwards and stretch, you are a starfish. Your mind calls this breathable. You sigh out loud, enough for someone to hear if they were beside you, and you inhale the fresh linen and rose oil. You are not thinking about failing. You are happy for eighteen seconds.

The salt lamp creates a loving red glow, and your arms are not pale, they are golden now. You will sleep. You nestle your head back, and your temples are enveloped by the goose-down pillow you bought from Amazon that smells like your bubblegum shampoo. You are a you-sandwich. You close your eyes and try to think only of your breathing. You do this for six minutes. You are happy for four of them.

You notice that you are peaceful because your teeth aren't clenched and your neck feels less sore now – this makes it OK to reach for your iPhone 7. The room becomes a sick blue, and your sheets reflect this up into your face, all bright and clinical. You are quote-tweeting an article from *The Atlantic* about Israel. 'Sorry, but Israel are c*nts,' you write.

You read more articles. You like more threads. You see that Julie's hand-inked drawing of a forlorn elephant has 108 retweets. You remember that your last illustration has only three likes. One from Julie, and two from your fake Twitter accounts, which you made to like your own illustrations. You pull up the screengrab of Julie's tweet from 2012 where she uses the N-word. You let the image hover there, loaded, with your finger on the reply button, but you don't post it, you delete it and post 'you are so fucking talented' under Julie's illustration instead.

You check your DMs and go on Instagram until it's 5.12 a.m. You are saving pictures of interior-design ideas for the house in your head. And you must get up now because you'd promised yourself that you'd wash your hair.

You commute on the DART and listen to a podcast about a serial killer. You like the bits about how the bodies are stored after they are murdered. And you think about being a serial killer, but not in a serious way – you just wonder if you'd be good at it. Your podcast is interrupted by a targeted advert which addresses your fertility.

Outside the moving DART it is all manic and sad purple with the rain droplets flashing that intrusive puce when a railway light is passed. The windows are foggy from the insides of other people's lungs, and you stop thinking about that because it's the type of thought that would make you need to get off the DART. When the track enters Tara Street station, Dublin darkens the cabin on either side with its laughing scaffold jaws. The frost wind is sideways this morning. The sky is garda-pants navy. You walk with your head bent and some cold wet enters your sock, and your earbuds are in, and you hope people won't look you in the eye. Your wet foot itches.

You arrive at your job in the design company, which you are only doing because you have a degree in graphic design from NCAD, which you didn't really want to do in the first place, but it's OK, you were seventeen. You are so angry and sad that you will never say that you are angry and sad, even out loud to yourself, because if you hear yourself say it, that will mean that it is real and you will cry. At work you design lunch menus for a carvery in Tallaght. You have forgotten what it's like to enjoy drawing. When you think this to yourself your teeth clench again and co-workers look at you all worried, and you know that your neck will hurt later. Your rent is €750 a month, but your room is very clean and tidy and there's a salt lamp. You'd like the bathroom to be cleaner but one of your housemates is from Tipperary. If you move back in with your parents in Ranelagh you won't feel like a real person.

You've started to really enjoy the taste of red wine. When it is five o'clock and nearing the end of work, you start to think about how red wines tastes. And you feel that this is OK because it just means that your palate is maturing and becoming sophisticated. In the Tara Street Centra you buy the bottle that has the little plastic bull on it. Bills collect around your feet as you push open the door of the apartment. You add them to the pile of unopened envelopes on the kitchen table. Your dinner is a steamed chicken breast with microwaved broccoli drizzled in a dressing made from cider vinegar and melted coconut oil. You eat this very rapidly, without breathing, so you can begin the wine.

You drink the wine on your bed and watch YouTube videos of Christina Aguilera singing in live situations where it's definitely her real voice and not assisted in any way. The wine is dry on your tongue, vinegary too, but not that vinegary because you had the cider vinegar with din-dins. The wine is all gone. You are annoyed with the empty wine bottle because it got drank so quickly. You wish you could have those big boxes of wine with taps on them that they sell in Australia. You are staring at the calendar of pugs on your wall. You are having an imaginary conversation in your head with Julie, except she looks more puggish in this fantasy, and she is very interested in what you have to say. You are at a party. Others are listening too, but not directly; they are listening with one ear because your words are so captivating it is distracting them from their conversations. You are talking to Julie about why it's so unfair that we can't buy big boxes of wine in Ireland. But then Julie says 'I've seen them in Lidl' and you feel furious that she would correct you like that while others are listening. Your teeth clench. You feel embarrassed for becoming so furious at a conversation with Julie that never happened, at a hypothetical party. That hot tearful sensation pokes behind your eyes. Sometimes the wine makes you happy, other times it makes you sad and angry. Tonight it's making you sad and angry. You check Twitter. Julie's illustration now has 2,567 retweets, because it has been featured in a Buzzfeed article called '30 Illustrators You Should Be Following on Twitter'. You open one of your other Twitter accounts, the one in a man's name – @George4321 – and you post the N-word tweet from 2012 under Julie's illustration of the elephant.

Afterwards, you feel small and pathetic and wish you hadn't done that. You begin to cry, and you tell yourself that you wouldn't like to be your friend if you weren't you. You catch a glimpse of yourself crying in the mirror and laugh at how red and wet your face is. The anger from the wine swirls into a type of destructive happiness when you remember that there is gin in the kitchen. It is not your gin. It's gin that your Tipperary housemate was given as a Christmas gift from work. You begin to drink the gin mixed with your half bottle of flat 7-Up.

You lie back on your Egyptian cotton sheets. You open your Bank of Ireland app. You have savings of €2,320 – mostly emergency money that your parents have given you over the years. You open Airbnb on your laptop. The landing page has an apartment in Barcelona with a balcony and a foreign-looking tree outside. Seeing this gives you a rush of purpose, happiness and meaning, a feeling that you had forgotten. You book it for Friday. You book it for two weeks – it is only €530 because it is October. You feel fucking amazing. This is the type of spontaneous decision you should have been making your whole life. You say this out loud as you take a large celebratory swig of neat gin straight from the bottle. You realise that you like drinking because it allows you to relive feelings from the past, like happiness and freedom, that you haven't really felt in several years. This particular thought is intensely depressing, and you are not ready to think like that, so you play S Club 7 on Spotify. You fall asleep with your earbuds in.

You wake up at 5 a.m. Spotify is now playing JLS. Your ear hurts from sleeping on it with the earbud in. There are three calm seconds where your mind is blank and confused. Then you remember the tweet. Then you remember Barcelona. You leap up in the bed. You are hungover and feel like one eye has gone wonky. You rip open the laptop to delete the N-word tweet under Julie's illustration. It's too late, others have screengrabbed your screengrab. You try to cancel the Airbnb. You see that it was only €530 because it cannot be cancelled and the money has been paid. You panic. You open Ryanair. The flights are €475. You buy them. You are now €1,005 deep.

You are in Barcelona. Your suitcase rumbles so loudly down the cobbles of La Rambla that the locals stare, so you lift the suitcase up in your arms – it is not that heavy because you didn't really pack. The weather isn't warm, but it's warmer than Dublin. And the sandstone is glowing golden on the pretty buildings, and the same golden buildings are a soothing blue from the morning moisture when they are in the distance. It reminds you of Monet's painting of Rouen Cathedral. Noticing this makes you feel hope. Everything is different here. There are bright green trees with waxy leaves that look fake with fat oranges between them. You have not returned the calls from work. If your father calls, you will tell him what is happening, but only if he calls.

You arrive at your apartment by using Google Maps. You worry about your data plan and open the last message from your host, Donald, on Airbnb. It reads, 'Beside the apartment there is a café. At the back, beside the toilet, is a little box that you must open with the app – turn on Bluetooth. Inside this box is the key for the apartment.' You retrieve the key and open the building door. Up the cold stairs. Your apartment is exactly as the pictures showed it. The doors are grainy mahogany, the floors are impossibly marble, there is a kitchen and a fridge. There are little windows with wooden shutters and the balcony with the big foreign tree. Everything is perfect and neat and clean. You want to keep it this way. The air smells like those candles from summer evening barbecues that keep away the midges – lemony but not lemon. You taste it when you sniff. You are not thinking about your design job, or Dublin, or Julie's forlorn elephant drawing. You are here, in Barcelona. You need this – you need to just be you, in Barcelona, with no plan. The recklessness of your decision makes you feel powerful.

You find a cute bar by Plaza del Porto. It is early evening now and the shadows are longer. The bar is playing Tame Impala and the waiting staff are all gorgeous and wearing black. You order the bottle of red that is €12 because you know that a €12 bottle of red wine here is really a €25 bottle back home. You are sitting at a small metal table outside in the evening sun. The wine tastes like a very complicated Ribena. You take a photo of the wine because you feel a placid optimism and want to preserve this feeling as a photo. You think about being very old, and dying on your own, and looking at the photo of the wine. This thought feels sad and frightening. So you drink a big gulp of the Ribena wine – you notice that big gulps taste less like Ribena. You are not ready to post about Barcelona to Instagram yet, so you don't.

A lad is looking at you. He has that look that lads have when they see women sitting on their own in bars. He says something. You think he's speaking Greek – it's definitely Greek. You smoke one of his cigarettes. He is younger than you. Drinking feels different when you do it with other people. You're shifting him now. His tongue is slightly intrusive and enthusiastic. The only English words he says are 'beauty', 'woman' and '*Game of Thrones*'. This is good enough. You both drink Jack Daniel's shots, and the barmaid doesn't even care if it overflows when she pours it. She is so cool and continental. The Greek has a face a bit like Justin Bieber from the nose up, a little bit, but has a very weak chin, and his breath smells like those small white things that you cough up sometimes and you don't know what they are or what they are for. You take selfies together just in case he's going to kill you.

He is fucking you now on the bed in your apartment. He is saying words that you don't understand. You can tell by where he keeps putting his hand that the words are probably about your anus. Your eyes are closed. You feel your forehead on the pillow, and you really would just like to cum and do a big scream. You think back to the green lights of the bar, where he was a bit like Justin Bieber from a certain angle. You don't really cum. You do a big scream anyway. This is good enough. The Greek leaves. It is 4.23 a.m. You go out to the balcony and smoke the fags he left, and you feel empty, but not as bad as the other empty you felt back in Dublin. This is more of a disappointed-in-yourself emptiness than a general existential emptiness. Emptiness is OK if there's a clear reason for it. Realising this feels kind of nice.

It is morning and Brenda texts you on WhatsApp.

'Amm where the fuck are you?'

'In Barcelona.'

'Okkk, questions aside for a moment. Tell me you have been watching the Julie Brosnan drama on twitter? OH MY GOD.'

'I have no internet here, sorry. Trying to be mindful of my data too.'

Brenda doesn't reply. You don't follow up. You tell yourself that Julie deserves this.

Donald, your Airbnb host, lives in the apartment next door. He hasn't messaged you much, only to give directions and provide the Wi-Fi code. It is clear that the apartment was once a very large space that has now been divided in two because, beyond your kitchen entrance, there is a little private outdoor area that is shared between both apartments. It has a washing machine that you can hear, and you listen to Donald walking around – he seems to wear flip-flops because his steps are slappy and loud. You assert that he is probably from generational money and inherited the apartment, and renting out one part as an Airbnb is how he makes a living. He has three reviews – they are all positive. The door to the private area has a sign in English that says 'private area, please, access prohibited'. This bothers you, and you have a bit of hangover fear – you don't like not knowing what is behind the door. You can't hear his feet anymore, so you very quietly unlatch the door, just to take a peek. The tiles are terracotta. Sure enough, there is a washing machine, and a washing line on which two identical blue blazers hang. Beyond this is an open door. The smell of cooking wafts from it, a shallot aroma. This makes you hungry. You see a little pan on the hob. This is the door to Donald's kitchen – you can hear his flip-flops pottering about in another part of the apartment. It is kind of funny, but you decide to slowly close the door so he doesn't catch you peeking. You've seen the private area now. It's OK, you can relax. As you pull away, a shadow steps into view against the visible wall of the kitchen beyond the frying pan. You stare for less than a second before you quietly shut the door.

You don't know how to fully describe to yourself what you just saw. The shadow did not appear to be human. It was short, roughly five feet, and rotund in a way that people are not. There was a protrusion about the face, like a beak or a bill, the legs were exceptionally skinny and the feet were large.

You begin to think about the two blue waistcoats on the washing line, and that your host's name is Donald, and that he made you collect the keys with an app instead of meeting you. You begin to entertain the idea that your temporary landlord may be Donald Duck. Not an anthropomorphic duck, existing in three dimensions, birthed fleshy into reality like at the end of the Halloween episode of *The Simpsons* where Homer walks down a real-life street. But rather a hand-painted animated two-dimensional Donald Duck, living in Barcelona, quietly renting out his apartment and tending to a pan of shallots.

Dublin does not matter anymore. Julie's forlorn elephant does not matter anymore. The N-word tweet does not matter anymore. The fuck with the Greek does not matter anymore. Your internal voice, which would usually interject and tell you that it is highly unlikely that your Airbnb host is a hand-painted animated duck, does not speak up. You don't search for rational explanations – that it was maybe just the warping of a shadow and you witnessed a completely unique and anomalous optical illusion, which you, and you alone, happened to see in one perfect moment, and this made a human's shadow appear as a famous cartoon duck. You cannot tell if this should worry you or, instead, if this reading of reality is something you truly need at this moment and shouldn't question. It doesn't feel frightening, it feels OK.

You imagine Donald next door. You place your palm on the wall to connect with him. You breathe, you listen to his slapping feet again and you pray for a quack. In your mind, you see his gigantic bulging eyes and his comically exasperated yellow beak, with the little navy sailor's cap tilted on his feathered head. A reclusive monstrosity in a dark Catalan apartment. Sadly attending to his fragrant shallots or whatever it was. You know what you saw. Poor lonely Donald.

You begin to think of the film *Who Framed Roger Rabbit*, where Bob Hoskins co-exists with two-dimensional cartoons. But even that did not look as real as this. Roger Rabbit never had a shadow – he was superimposed.

You worry about having seen something that you can never tell another person. You've just left your job and gone to Barcelona without alerting anyone. They are all going to have questions back home, and you will need to have decent answers – about stress or depression or something. Your family will be worried. You've most likely lost your job. Your former co-workers will contact you on Facebook. You explaining that your Airbnb host is a fully animated two-dimensional cartoon duck is exactly what they'd expect to hear. You imagine Julie hearing this, and her feeling superior and saying things like, 'Well, she probably can't even draw him, so I don't know how she saw him, hahahaha,' and then she'd post a passive-aggressive hand-inked illustration of a well-drawn duck on her Behance page, which would get many shares. You refuse to let that happen.

The morning is warm and smells of flowers you don't know. You walk down the wide Barcelona street, marvelling at how each road leads to a square intersection and how every inter-section has a little bodega or café where smiling people eat breakfasts. You don't want to meet any other Irish people here: this is yours. You play the song 'Fantasy' by Mariah Carey on your Spotify, and you really feel it, every crescendo of her voice, the effortless blend of hip-hop and R&B. Your walk becomes a little dance. You are happy, you notice that you are happy and this makes you even more happy, and then that makes you feel a sense of meaning. Fuck purple Dublin.

You sit down at a table and drink a coffee, and instead of milk, there's a sweet magnolia syrup that tastes like toffee. And the coffee is in a glass, like an upside-down Guinness, with the creamy white syrup at the bottom and the thick black coffee on top – they are two lovers refusing to talk. You mix them with the little cheerful spoon, and the syrup and coffee dance together. They swirl their black and yellow argument into a beige infusion like clouds in a tempest. This reminds you of the paintings of William Turner. You feel very creative when you notice that you noticed this. And you crunch slices of just-baked hot toasted bread between your teeth, with a spread made from fresh tomatoes and butter. It is delicious. And you have a sherry for breakfast, fuck it.

You walk into an art shop and you buy those large tubes of acrylic paint, the really big ones, and you buy brushes and pens.

And you go to a printing shop, and you point at Ao-sized sheets of see-through plastic. They are almost as big as you when you hold them up. You buy fifteen of them. This costs €300. You don't care. They roll them up in two poster tubes and you carry them under each arm.

Back at the apartment, you imagine that Donald Duck is lonely, on his own, eating shallots. Locked in a prison. Never able to meet a human. Having his items delivered. Terrified of the brutal violence that would be done to him if an animated cartoon duck were to venture out into the real world. You want to make a wife for him.

You think back to your animation module in college. How animations are made of cels – see-through plastic sheets with little movements of a character placed on them. And when the sheets are placed on each other fast enough, the human eye sees this as movement, and this is what a cartoon is.

In your sketchpad you try to design a female duck, but drawing ducks is so much harder than you thought, so instead it is a platypus, which also has a beak but is essentially just a big circle with a flat tail. Her name is Maura. She has long eyelashes. Her beak ends in voluptuous red lips. She wears bicycle shorts because dresses are also difficult to draw. And she has one of those long cigarettes to make her classy. Maura the platypus, she is bright pink.

It is night now. You have been drawing Maura all day.

The Greek is shouting 'Westeros' outside your window. You go to the balcony, and he is wearing a 1975 T-shirt and is looking up at you like an elbow-chinned Romeo. You bring the Greek into your apartment. He points and says things about all the paint and paper. You take him away from them and bring him into the bedroom. There is multicoloured dry acrylic paint all over your legs. You take your T-shirt and shorts off and get up on the bed with your head in the pillow so that you don't smell his breath. He begins fucking and saying things that you don't understand, probably about your anus. It is good enough. You realise that he can't understand you either, so you say, 'My landlord is Donald Duck.' The Greek says things in response and keeps looking at your anus. So then you shout it: 'My fucking landlord is Donald Duck. He's a big white cartoon duck, and he's next door now.' When you say this, the sex feels a lot better. So you keep shouting: 'Fuck me, you weak-chinned Greek dork. Fuck into me really hard. My landlord is a giant famous animated duck and he'd probably kill you if you had a fight.' The Greek shouts things too, probably about your anus because he's trying to edge his thumb towards there. You don't like this and bat his hand away. He feels embarrassed by this so pumps harder as a form of compromise. You think of the split second when he looked like Justin Bieber under the green light. You cum and he leaves. The bit at the end felt really great.

At night you paint Maura on the giant A0 see-through plastic sheets that you bought from the printing shop. You have drawn and painted only her body on one main cel. On the other cels you paint an arm and tail. In each cel her arm slowly rises with her long cigarette, while her pink platypus tail flaps down. Each night you let the Greek in and then he leaves. He is not permitted to see Maura. He is being weird about this. You close the living-room door and he is only allowed into the bedroom. Sometimes he wants to stay, but you don't let him. He washes acrylic paint out of his balls in the kitchen sink.

Eight nights have passed now.

You only care about Donald and Maura.

You work at night, silently, because you can access the private area with the washing machine and the clothes line while Donald is asleep. You will not message him, even though the shower has gone cold. You don't need showers. There is paint on the floors, the doors, the microwave, the bed – he will understand. Every morning you smell his cooking shallots and hear his giant duck feet slap around his kitchen. When this happens you touch the wall and your heart feels full, and you think of love and not being afraid. You have a purpose now.

On the tenth night you hang Maura's cels on the washing line in the private area. You have threaded the cels through the line so they pass over each other. The paintwork is solid and opaque, no brush strokes. Maura the platypus hangs pink. When you pull the twine of the washing line, the cels pass over each other quick enough to create a three-second animation. They make whirring noises. You light it with your phone torch. Her hand rises to her mouth with her long cigarette and then her tail flaps. She exists, with the washing machine behind her. She is almost real. It needs something more. You paint additional cels so that her eye winks and seductive smoke trails from the red lips on her beak. You sit back on the ground with the washing-line twine in each hand, pulling and tugging. Watching her over and over. Drinking great red wine. Maura is the perfect wife.

You realise that you have created a piece of art. Better than fucking Julie with her online illustrations. You have made an installation. A two-dimensional hand-painted platypus, hanging on a washing line, that is fully animated when you pull the strings and each cel overlaps. She moves in reality.

It is the eleventh night.

You have Maura and all her cels set up on the washing line now. It is 4 a.m. Donald will awake in a few hours and cook his shallots. He will look out into the private area and no longer feel alone. His pink cartoon wife will flap her tail, and wink at him, and blow her smoke. He will see her. His shallot monotony will end. He will have a two-dimensional animated companion. He will be happy.

At 6.39 a.m. you get two WhatsApps from Brenda.

'What the actual fuck are you doing over in Barcelona?'

'Why are people sharing videos on pornhub of you riding some greek lad and roaring about donald duck? What are you doing over there?'

There is a link to the video in the text. You watch the video. It is you. You feel your heart in your throat. You rush into the bedroom and frantically look around. Then you see it. Under the ceiling fan. The little reflective glimmer of a lens. Your Airbnb host has been recording you with a hidden camera. Donald and Maura no longer matter.

River otters are larger. They can be recognised by their rotund ears. They Are FROM TUAM

BELOW IN JOEY RAMONE

My name is Coffin. My teeth are chalky and my skin is like a chameleon that is translucent. My violet veins pulse underneath – they bulge in a way that casts shadows on my wrists. I keep my hair standing up using green house paint, the type you'd put on the plaster wall of a parlour or a living room, not the shiny oily kind you'd paint onto wood that smells like pine. I call myself a punk, but I don't look like any of the punks you've seen in photographs. In the 1970s in Askeaton there were only four punks: me and my brothers Gorta, Nipple and Gossun.

I speak a language that is unique to me, in an accent that is unique to me. It has hissing and clicking noises, in a way that no Gaelic or English is uttered in Ireland. It is my own thing. You can't hear it. But I'll compensate for this with very animated gestures from my arms and face. If you care enough to listen, you will understand me perfectly. I spit when I speak. My spit is coloured bright green from the paint in my hair, and if you wear good clothes when you are near me, your shirt will have specks of colour on it.

Askeaton is a small town that clenches like crooked teeth. Once a year in May, shoals of brown trout try to swim up the River Deel, but they die on the banks under the bridge, so the whole town stinks of hot fish and becomes overrun with fat otters who'll bite your knees and won't let go until they hear a bone snap. So everyone wears wellies with twigs in them and runs from house to house in case they see a quare otter.

Me and my brothers lived in a limestone cottage two miles to the back of Askeaton, impenetrably surrounded by thick briars and ash trees. A briar is a bastard of a thing. It's like a commune of bristly hedges. If you showed me a briar patch, I couldn't tell you if it was one big massive bush sprawling out or hundreds of them all tangled up. They have thorns like new penknives on the branches – if you could call them branches – and the cuts they give sting for hours and glow red. They'd get infected too. A briar patch is the closest thing you'd have to lava or quicksand in Ireland. Not as deadly, more annoying than deadly, but still to be avoided. So, my cottage was surrounded by them. For acres I tell you. You could only access the area via one specific tunnel through the thorny briars, and you'd need a hatchet and knowledge of the twists and turns to get there. No one got as far as our cottage, only me and my brothers. And I'll use great swoops of my arms and legs to tell you this, I'll re-enact creeping and hacking movements with my eyes closed.

The immediate land around our cottage was dotted with the skulls of other cottages that were no more, just their markings in the grass. Only the crows above looking down could make out the shapes of the buildings that might have stood. They were gone for over a hundred years. The land had the faint traces of a few roads and a bump that was once a water pump. In summer, the grass where the roads were would bloom with bright red poppies, and the pollen would rise up like ghosts in the evening sun. This is how you'd know where the small streets and alleys once were paved.

After the Great Famine, it was the case that an entire village in rural Limerick might disappear. Every person who lived there, every person who'd ever visited, would be gone suddenly. And so the hungry briars would crawl over and stretch their way along the earth, finding their thorns in between the cobbles and whitewash, slowly tearing down everything that once was until it was nothing. Only briar.

No person in Askeaton knew the name of the dead village where we lived, or that it ever existed, or that it was even there, only me and my brothers, and I will not tell you how we came to live there, because I'm not too sure myself. But I have a feeling now, at this stage in my life, that we were born there and came from a single family who stayed in that village since the 1840s – isolated from the rest of Ireland, uncontacted and reclusive. This would explain our odd speech and language.

We had attained a type of self-sufficiency in the dead village. We farmed kale and ate worms or captured crows and magpies. We fished for trout, because there was the shkelp of a stream to the west. We had nettles too and we boiled thistle when the kale was gone.

In 1979, an American boy from New Jersey found our cottage. He was roaming the countryside of Limerick for traces of his people and his search led him to our dead village. There he met me and my brothers. He was the only other person who had heard of the village but could not pronounce its name and referred to it as Gordaborenaheeky. The boy said that his great-great-great-grandmother was born there as a child.

The boy's mannerisms were jittery, and his arms and face shook when he spoke. He explained that he suffered greatly from shyness and apologised before every third sentence. He wore bright pink hair, spiked up high, and had safety pins in his ears and skinny torn denims with patches on them.

We believed that his ripped clothes were from crawling through the briars, but the boy explained that he was a punk. He told us about punks in America and about listening to the Ramones and the Damned and the Sex Pistols. He showed us Polaroid photos of him and his punk friends in New Jersey, standing against walls, posing, being bowzy. We had never put eyes on a photograph before, and so we grabbed at them and wouldn't give them back. This made the boy even more anxious. And his fear became a type of standing fit. The brothers and me were enamoured. We asked him questions about every detail of his life, we touched his hands and legs, we asked about each item of clothing and jewellery on him, we got up close and tried to smell his breath and hair, we asked him to stay and live with us, but the boy became frozen. 'Desprit frozen, like a whinny hare what done seen up inty the sun,' as my brother Gossun said at the time. So then the boy, he ran away through the briars and all we were left with was his memory.

From then on, all the brothers and myself would ever speak about to each other was the brightly coloured Yank and the day he visited. At first in passing. Then it became continuous. Then it became an obsession. We believed the American to be a type of heroic forest spirit who would one day return to us and lead us into a great battle. We began to arrange bits of twigs and sticks into the shape of the boy and dressed it up with poppies and dandelions and grass. And soon we had a type of straw punk American boy that we mounted on the bump where the town pump once stood. We would offer the effigy kale because on the day the boy visited we had been roasting kale root and thought this smell may have drawn him in.

Every evening we would re-enact the conversation with the boy in as much detail as possible. Each brother would take a turn and talk like an American through the effigy. We would recreate his nervous speech, his New Jersey accent and his jittery hand and face movements, eventually forming this into a type of dance. Each of us would tell great stories about Joey Ramone, Johnny Rotten, Sid Vicious and Doc Martens, but with no context as to what or who these things actually were, while the other brothers would listen with wide eyes and open mouths to the thrill and excitement of the day that the Yank came.

On nights of storytelling, Syg Vishish became a great pike below in Lough Gur who guarded the ghost of a banshee. When Syg Vishish would open her mouth you could see directly into hell. Any man who saw this would go mad and kill themselves. Dog Mairtens was a type of all-knowing fungus that stretched under the earth and kept the briars from growing into your throat as you slept. Joiny Roddin was a trickster spirit who on autumn nights would cover the stars with his infinite hands. When I'd tell the brothers about Joiny Roddin, I would flutter my arms in their faces, so it would look like several arms, and I'd nearly knock the Benson out of Nipple's mouth.

Over time details would change. The Yank became eighteen-foot tall with shoulders as big as geese and arms made from the mountains and saliva from all the rivers in Ireland and eyes carved from jewels stolen from pine martens. Thunderstorms became intense battles between Joiny Roddin and the brightly coloured Yank, fighting for ownership of the day and night.

We buried the stolen Polaroids of the New Jersey punks under the trunk of a dead oak tree. We believed that the photographs were little frozen humans, rendered immovable by ice, and that any warmth would cause the figures to leap out of the picture. If this event were to ever happen, our bodies would turn inside out, and the little figures would drag us like cattle through the briars, and we'd be forced to wander Ireland for eternity in search of a cure for the wounds. So the photos could only be dug up on a bitter night of great frost and each brother would let a pint of blood onto the oak trunk before even attempting to break the cold soil with a rock. On these nights we would study the Polaroids fiercely, memorising the punk clothes and the hairstyles, careful not to warm the figures with the flame of the torch.

The conversations with the straw Yank became a ceremony. The Polaroids became relics. It gave us meaning and entertainment. It gave us purpose in the isolation of the dead village.

We began to call ourselves punks and we named our dead village Joey Ramone. And if even so much as a strong gust rustled the briars, we would look towards the opening with the hearts thumping in our chests in the hopes that the Yank would return.

We began to dress like punks so that he might come back. But we had no way to procure punk clothes, so we would paint punk clothes onto our naked bodies, based on the frozen glimpses of the buried photographs.

We would wait until the darkest nights, when Joiny Roddin had his hands stretched over the stars and moon. And we'd light torches made from straw and oil from pine bark and move through the briars until we reached Askeaton town, hissing and clicking in our own tongue. The trips to Askeaton were a terrifying affair for myself and the brothers, which would take weeks of planning. We became masters of evasion. We did not trust the people of Askeaton with their cars and phone boxes. We believed the Askeaton people to be an evil fairy race who would eat us if they ever found us or the village of Joey Ramone. The brothers and me would tell ourselves that the great pike Syg Vishish would swim up the Deel to protect us on these trips and open her mouth to show the torture pits of hell to any Askeaton warrior who'd try to eat us. We would smash the front window of Keanes' hardware shop on Church Street and steal tins of house paint and spill it on the cobbles. And the whole town would be so confused whenever this would happen.

We kept a pig for warmth in the limestone cottage of Joey Ramone. By the way I remember the pig, I'd wager that it was an extremely inbred wild boar and not a pig at all – an animal long extinct from the wilds of Limerick but somehow descended from a tame Famine boar. But we called it the pig.

Pigs have skin like people. So we began painting the pig like how the Yank described the punks, to see which paint would stick to the skin and not wash off if it rained. We settled on vinyl matt emulsion.

And so I painted my legs blue like drainpipe jeans and painted a string vest on my torso that said 'The Damned'. The brothers did similar, but the colours were not bright and vivid – they were muted and pastel because we were using house paints intended for walls and not fashion.

Me and the brothers had also never heard punk music, so we would make our own using clapping and our voices and hollow flutes fashioned from hard mud dried in a fire. All of our punk songs would be performed in the cottage, and the only audience was the pig. Most of the songs were about the pig, but some were about the Yank and Joiny Roddin and Syg Vishish.

In winter in Askeaton there's a wet wind in off the mountains. So me and the brothers would paint more clothes on ourselves. One brother painted himself heavy leather boots that went all the way up to his knees. Another painted a long leather trench coat with a fur lining.

It was my belief that the act of painting yourself in heavy clothing was enough to ward off the wet mountain wind. I would say that weather is clever, not just a dumb force but a form of intelligence, and that you could choose to disobey it or obey it. This is why we kept a pig for warmth instead of lighting a fire: to confuse the cold. This is why me and the brothers would paint our clothes onto our naked skin: to confuse the wet wind.

One September, my brother Gossun died of paint. He had covered all of his body in emulsion. The skin is an organ and if you paint your entire body you will slowly suffocate. Under his drainpipe jeans and leather jacket he had painted leggings and a thermal vest. On his face he had painted the face of another man, a better-looking man he had once seen in Askeaton. He had left no inch of his skin without emulsion paint. And so he died.

When he died, we painted Gossun a hole in the ground at the back of the cottage and painted the body the same colour as the hole, and the body just disappeared.

After the death of Gossun, the ceremonies with the straw Yank became different. Gossun's spirit had absorbed into the Yank and would sometimes talk to us through the Yank. Gossun's ghost would tell us that if we did not broker a peace with the town of Askeaton, we would all soon die. This brought a great fear upon us. We were certain that the people of Askeaton would eat us as we stood. So we made ourselves inedible. We began to mix our own piss, vomit, shit and blood into the tins of vinyl matt emulsion. And we would paint ourselves up like punks with tall bright hair. We would walk through Askeaton town together during the day time, stinking to high heaven. To our surprise, no one tried to eat us. In fact, people actively avoided us. We had figured out a type of armour that kept the hungry Askeaton fairy race at bay.

So we grew bold. We now visited Askeaton to bring terror. Our fear of being eaten had turned into a type of entitled loathing. No more covert night-time expeditions through the briars with pine torches. We were proud and cocky and painted like shitty pissy bloody punks.

We would go on raids. We would scatter through the local shop like a group of bowld terriers and steal sweets, biscuits and crisps to bring back through the briars to Joey Ramone and offer at the feet of the straw Yank. We became contemptuous of the people of Askeaton, seeing them as a lesser race who feared us. We started to learn their language and the power structure of Askeaton town.

We would stand on the corner of Church Street watching everything – the post office, the bank, the Fine Gael office. And people hurried past us with handkerchiefs over their mouths. I chased down the priest, Father Casey, and stole the collar from his neck, which I then wore as an amulet. A spoil of war. We began stealing money from people. At first, we didn't know what money was, but careful watching and listening educated us of its power over others.

We would snatch handbags or spit on men and take their wallets. We observed that money came from the bank, so we tracked down the manager, Pontious McNamara, and we stole his patent leather shoes and tore the buttons from his shirt, leaving him helpless in the town fountain. This was a stretch too far and so the sergeant intervened. He bashed me over the head with a truncheon. This put manners on us. We returned to our cottage in Joey Ramone, apprehensive again about our trips to Askeaton.

Without the Askeaton raids, myself and Gorta and Nipple were short of money and crisps and Fanta. So we painted the pig to look like the bank manager and changed his name to Pontious McNamara the Bank Manager. Pontious would give us loans of money whenever we required it – ash-tree leaves painted to look like banknotes. And we would take sacks of the money to Askeaton town. We would tell the shopkeeper that the money was given to us by Pontious McNamara, and the shopkeeper would exchange it for crisps, biscuits and Fanta. It was effectively working for us as legal tender. But I reckon the shopkeeper was willing to part with a few sweets just to get the three naked men painted in their own bodily fluids out of the shop.

The cottage became cold without the pig being a pig, but the money allowed us to buy wood for the fire.

My brother Nipple once borrowed too much money and

couldn't pay it back. So we took the problem to the straw Yank, and the Yank and the pig ruled that Nipple be killed, and so myself and Gorta killed him with sticks. And we painted him into the same grave that Gossun was buried in. And his body disappeared.

Then it was only me and my brother Gorta left. Pontious McNamara soon came asking both of us to return the money that he had loaned us as bank manager. Myself and Gorta feared that we would have to kill each other if the bank manager decided that this was how the debt should be repaid. We kept this a secret from the straw Yank and we took it upon ourselves to paint Pontious McNamara in his sleep, so that he would stop being a bank manager and go back to being a pig. But Pontious had spent so much time as a bank manager that we had forgotten what pigs look like, so when we painted him, it was not a pig but the memory of a pig. It was a new creature. One that hadn't the benefit of millions of years of evolution. It could not eat. It could not move. It was just a very strange pink creature with sad little eyes and a large mouth and curly tail. The creature had trotters painted from memory. They were very sharp. The creature would thrash violently about the cottage and try to slit its own throat with its sharp trotters. But its legs were too short to reach. So me and Gorta painted longer legs, and the creature killed itself. We painted the creature's body into the hole with Gossun and Nipple and it disappeared.

I was lonely, so Gorta painted himself into a woman. He painted a woman's body and woman's underpants, and a bra on his chest. And I painted a wedding suit onto myself. And we got married in Lough Gur with the blessing of the pike Syg Vishish.

At first our marriage was pleasant, but I began to drift with a horn on me and painted the straw Yank into a mistress. My wife discovered this and was heartbroken, so she beheaded the mistress and painted herself back into Gorta. And it was just me and Gorta again. No Gossun, no Nipple, no straw Yank, no pig. Just lonely old bachelors in a limestone cottage surrounded by briar.

By that time it was the 1990s, and both of us were in our mid-fifties. So we painted ourselves as younger men and began taking trips beyond the cottage into Askeaton again. We would mix emulsion paint into a type of bright pink to give our skin youth. And we would paint more clearly defined muscles on each other. Gorta said we looked like young hunks. And the local girls below in the town in their twenties would go wild. They would follow and chase the two of us from one end of Askeaton town to the other, enamoured with our beauty and handsomeness, tearing the shirts and dresses off themselves. The girls of Askeaton had never seen such beautiful men. And women would have their hearts broken and would fight over us in the town square, and they would beg me and the brother to get them pregnant and marry them. This attention was too much for us. We thought that youth and female attention would bring us happiness, but instead it made us more lonely.

So we stayed clear of Askeaton once again and returned to the solitude of the cottage in Joey Ramone. We painted ourselves as white clouds and we painted the grass around our cottage like a June sky, bright blue, with the tins we had left. We moved slowly together, palms interlocked, creeping with our feet. Two white lumps drifting through the chalky blue grass each day, painted like massive cumulus clouds floating high up in the stratosphere. This slow, silent humility brought us the peace we had craved all along. No more did we wait for a Yank to lead us into battle.

We came to realise that by becoming the sky we had no need for food, water, love or attention. Just slow steady movements. Drifting and rolling through the blue grass.

Our impression of the sky was so convincing and hypnotic that it confused the wildlife of Askeaton, in particular the birds. And soon our cottage and all of Joey Ramone was black with gulls and rooks and sparrows, silently watching. Occasionally a wren might try and fly towards the bright blue grass, to no avail. After two weeks the cats followed the birds, and the dogs followed the cats. They had all relocated to the spectacle of the creeping cloud brothers. There were no birds to eat the insects of Askeaton – we, the two painted brothers, were the only focus of the avians. Bees began to sting below in Askeaton, and midges went wild, and dinners were ruined with flies. Butchers' shops were cleared out from maggots. No bird had any business in the town. So the locals followed the birds and cut away the briars and found the two of us painted as clouds, and they found our cottage, and they found Joey Ramone. And they sent us off to be fixed.

TOBY

1.17 a.m. Gus Slattery, 21, is angrily returning home from Cormac Denehy's house near Sarsfield Barracks. They are prominent members of the Catholic Society of Mary Immaculate College, where they are both studying to become teachers. There was an argument and Gus was asked to leave Cormac's house.

Maybe if Denehy wasn't such a cynic he'd have the gumption to speak to her. That's what it was about and make no mistake of it. He has no bother on him ringing me on a Sunday with the fear when he's not feeling the best. I was right to slap him – he had it coming. It wasn't even a proper punch. I felt the side of his stringy head on my palm. It was a slap, not a real dig, and he'll get over it. That's it. Knowing him, he has the puss on him now. 'Gus can't be disagreed with. He's a bully. You saw how he reacted. We should bring it up with Father Purcell – I think he's drifting away from the values we hold dear.' And Emma will be like, 'Ohhh, ohhh, the side of your face is so red, Cormac. Have you any ice in the freezer? Or even peas would do?' And she'll have the peas out against his big Longford forehead, and they'll listen to Kings of Leon, and they can't be trusted, and he'll use that moment to coax her into different types of filth that he probably had planned all along.

1.18 a.m. Declan Nevin, 33, office worker, lies on his single bed in a house on Nicholas Street. His landlady's dog is barking below in the kitchen. The house is an old terraced brick tenement with a grey roof that weeps in the middle, underneath which is a converted attic where Declan lodges because the Latvian wife had enough of his whinging.

What if I put the pillow like this, over my head, like, and do that with the other one underneath? Is that mould on the pillow? No, I can still fucking hear him. Is this punishment? Is that what this is? What I wouldn't give to just be beside her in the nice big bed. As the man says, happy as Larry I'd be. No fucking barking, no springs sticking into my calf. The warmth of her back against my chest. The smell of her neck. Oh, shut the fuck up you little cur. Yapping, yapping, yapping. He's fed, he's watered, he's been let out. What could have him barking at this hour?

1.18 a.m. Toby, 7, a Jack Russell terrier, is barking downstairs in the kitchen of Nicholas Street. Toby feels anxious – he does not know why. He is aware that he has been fed, watered and let out, but is experiencing a malaise.

Bark, bark, bark, bark.

1.19 a.m. Gus Slattery has turned a corner off Barrack Street.
The houses get smaller now. The night has a chilly dryness to it.
The moon is neon cornflower on the tarmac and in the puddles
from earlier.

I bet they're shifting, I fucking know it. My own fault, sure. If
I hadn't slapped Denehy then they wouldn't be shifting each
other now. You brought this one on yourself, Augustine, the
self-fufilling prophecy again. What if they ride? Oh, Lord above.
No, they wouldn't ride. Emma isn't like that. But what if he
feels her tit? Oh, the conniving bollocks. Cormac Denehy with
his Longford hands breaching the stiff wire of Emma Clancy's
bra, and his fucking bogman's fingertips on her nipples. Her
perfect pink nipples, or maybe they're brown? No, she wouldn't
have brown ones – they'd be pink and pure, like little rabbits'
noses. And the golden crucifix between them, the cold metal
Lord flanked by warm tits. No no no. No room for thoughts like
that. Cop on now, Augustine. Maybe she left the house? Maybe,
maybe she left to follow me because when I slapped Denehy it
drove up a passion in her? She saw who the real man was, and
she's searching the streets for me. With red cheeks and cold air
from her lips. The innocence on her. Ready to say that she needs
me, that she'd rather die than be without me, that she'll obey me
and never hurt me. Should I go back, maybe? No, no, no way.
She's fucking shifting him, get real. She has her tongue in his
mouth now. And she's thinking about doing more. Oh, Christ
above, why did I allow this to happen?

1.20 a.m. Declan Nevin is still trying to sleep above in Nicholas Street. He is thinking about his wife.

Four hours? I suppose I could get by on four hours' sleep. Ya, didn't I read before that Thatcher used to sleep for four hours, and she ran a country, sure. As the man says, she made fucking shit of the mines, but that was more due to the ould cunty humour on her than the sleep, I'd say. Ya, it will be fine. I'll pull into the Starbucks by the monument just after 6 a.m., get a double espresso in me, small drop of milk, ham-and-cheese croissant. And I'll have ten minutes in the jacks of the office before anyone gets in, in case the espresso gives me the scutters. Not a bother on me.

I wonder what Lasma is doing? She does the skin thing before bed tonight, isn't it? Should I give her a text and say I saw the Elizabeth Arden stuff on sale in Debenhams? Maybe buy it and there's an excuse to drop over tomorrow? I'll give her one text. No, stop, Declan, stop. Self-control. Show her that you can exist without needing her. That would wake her up anyway, it'd make things worse. Oh, Jesus. Will he shut up, shut up!

1.20 a.m. Toby is anxious.

Bark, bark, bark.

1.21 a.m. Gus Slattery has stopped at the foot of Nicholas Street. There is a well-practised scowl behind his thick glasses. Long shadows move across the pebble-dashed walls when he avoids puddles to protect the suede Dubarrys on his feet. His phone creates a pale glow.

I'll need to have some story for Father Purcell because Denehy will be straight in to him by the morning, telling on me over the slap. There will be instructions that I need to go on a retreat with the Cistercians in Kildimo, to hand my anger over to the spirit, and he'll tell me about Our Lord turning cheeks and why slapping other men is wrong. What could I say to him, like? 'I'm sorry, Father Purcell, but we are both madly in love with Emma Clancy, and neither of us will say it to each other, or to her. So we met up in Denehy's flat to drink cups of tea and discuss raising money for Milford Hospice, and Denehy was clearly making suggestions for me to leave so he could have Emma to himself, so then I showed them a video on YouTube of a man who turned his dead cat into a drone, and an altercation escalated from there. I'm so sorry, Father.' I wouldn't even have to get into the bit about Padre Pio, but I'm sure Denehy would find a way to tell him, and then there'd be all sorts of shit to deal with.

1.22 a.m. There is a chill in the room above in Nicholas Street. Toby barks. Declan Nevin knows that if he takes out his phone to look at his ex-wife's Facebook then he most definitely will not sleep. He is feeling angry about his landlady.

Of course, if it woke her below, she'd be quick to get that dog to shut up. Fine rent she has me charged and all. No chance of dropping twenty bob due to the dog, like. She has herself up to the gant in Valium downstairs in the bed. She thinks I don't see the packets in the biscuit tin behind the cornflakes. Off her tits on Vallys, as the man says. She must have them counted out because there's no way a doctor will give her more, unless she's lying to multiple doctors about how much she needs. The dog's not doing a thing to her fucking sleep.

Lasma is hardly riding anyone, is she? She wouldn't do that. Not in public anyway. We're still married sure. It's only been two months. But what if she's riding on the quiet? The Irwin's lad next door? He's nineteen, isn't he? Big rugby player chest on him. Oh bollix, what if he's hopping the back wall and going in the sliding doors so no one sees and they're riding like mad? In our bed. Stop it. Stop that type of thinking now. What did we say the other night about the jealousy, Declan? Fuck it, she probably needs the ride. If it made her happy. What harm if it meant she was happy. I deserve this. I took her for granted.

Oh, shut up, Toby. Can I not at the very fucking least feel sorry for myself in silence? What if I gave him the landlady's Valium? Even a quarter of one? She wouldn't miss it then. I'm fourteen stone, which means I could take two, and I'd wager that he's just under one stone. So I could give him an eighth of one, and it might put him to sleep for the few hours we've left. That sleeping dragon downstairs mightn't notice if I just took a bit off a pill.

1.22 a.m. Toby is moving from the door into the kitchen to the other door that leads to the back garden. The sound of his own claws on the lino is painful to his ears. There is an energy in him that feels misdirected and unspent. He senses that this will be alleviated by going out into the garden. He is unsure if this will satiate his anxiety fully but is willing to try. When he hears his own claws again, this excites him, and he expresses this as a nervous bark.

Bark, bark ... bark, bark.

1.23 a.m. Gus Slattery has begun to walk down Nicholas Street. His phone is put away, and there is a worry upon him. His phone beeps – it is an email from Denehy. His phone is in his hand again.

'Myself and Emma are both shook, Gus. The way you behaved tonight was completely at odds with the values of the Society. We must, at all times, surrender ourselves to the Catholic doctrine, in our speech, in our actions, in our thoughts, in how we treat each other. What you did tonight was anything but reflect these values. I'm drafting a letter to Father Purcell with a recommendation for your expulsion from the group. I'm sorry, but just to be upfront and transparent. Here's what I've written:

> *Dear Father Purcell,*
> *Earlier tonight, Emma Clancy and Gus Slattery joined me in my flat to have a discussion about raising funds for the sick and dying of Milford Hospice. Gus made a comment that caused both Emma and I to feel deeply uncomfortable. He began by showing us a video of a German man who had converted his recently deceased cat into a drone, a type of small helicopter-like object, which is controlled remotely. But in this video, the preserved body of a house cat was stretched over the drone. So it appeared to be a flying cat. While this video was quite immature, and both Emma and I found the disrespect for the cat's remains, as a creature of God, to be inappropriate, this was sadly not the worst of his behaviour.*
> *Gus Slattery, for the record, found this video hilarious. Forgive me for what I say next, but Gus Slattery then suggested that the corpse of the blessed Padre Pio be made*

*into a drone and asked us both what we would think of
that. He then laughed maniacally, as if taking pleasure in
our shock. Emma and I were aghast at this "joke", this sick,
twisted comment. I, rightfully, called Gus out on this immediately. To which he then responded with physical violence.
He was possessed with a demonic rage. He clenched his fist
and hit me directly in the mouth with all his force, knocking
me back. He then stood over me, with menace and threat in
his eyes, and began calling me names I won't repeat.*

*I am OK, but Emma is very upset by this and, as a young
woman, should not have witnessed this savagery. I am
writing this letter to request that Gus Slattery be disciplined
and expelled from the Catholic Society of Mary Immaculate
College. I apologise for sending such a disturbing email to
you, Father, but I feel it is the correct thing to do.*

*Yours faithfully,
Cormac Denehy'*

Oh, the big streaky Longford fucking prick. Milford Hospice
my hole. He invited her over to coerce her into filth. And then
I only came along to protect her innocence from him. I knew
he'd do this, I knew it. It was just a slap. One slap on the side of
his head, the bony part. There was no closed fist. My arse did
she sign off on that letter either. The dangly liar. There was no
'menace or threat'. I did it to protect Emma. Yes, to protect her.
Good man, Augustine.

The video was funny – Emma laughed at it. I know this because
she looked directly at me. With the way her mouth creases and
her eyes sparkle when she laughs. And her and I had a private

little moment, and we both wished he'd be gone, and then the jealous grunt saw that. And it made me uncomfortable.

And when I went in with the joke about the Padre Pio drone – for Emma's entertainment, not his – he saw this as a threat and used it to embarrass me with words. Up on his fucking high horse, getting offended. I slapped him. And the opportunist kicked me out. Told me I wasn't welcome, with no thought as to what druggy types might be lurking in the streets I now walk.

He deserved the slap, and I'd do it again. This is a ruse. That's what this is. He has her to himself now. He is culling me. Poisoning me. Poisoning her. Poor innocent Emma, with her warm red lips and eyes that wouldn't know a badness in them. The way the curls of hair on her forehead stick to the skin with sweat and it takes all of my restraint not to brush them away. Her gentle Thurles lilt leaving her lips. She's imprisoned inside in Denehy's evil plot and probably doesn't even know she needs rescuing. The poor thing. She deserves so much better than this. And no doubt he has her bra off now, and he's forcing her hand down his stupid beige corduroys, and he's using their 'intimacy' to plant things in her head about me and she's too innocent to know different. The big Longford snake.

1.25 a.m. Declan Nevin is creeping down the wooden ladder from the attic of his landlady's house on Nicholas Street. He is naked from the waist down. His belly is hard and round from nightly porter. His legs are white, hairy and thin. He wears a faded Star Wars *T-shirt. He turns the knob on the old heavy door that leads into the kitchen, which has that cheese smell from Toby's hair.*

Pss, psss psss, pss, c'mere, Toby. Good lad. Don't be licking my fucking feet – you've a fixation on exposed feet. Shut up and keep away from my feet.

1.25 a.m. Toby hears Declan descending the stairs. He is no longer anxious. He wiggles, he is almost sick with excitement at the prospect of Declan opening the door. He sees that Declan is barefoot and proceeds to lick his toes because foot skin tastes salty and Toby enjoys this small pleasure.

Hahaha, slup slup, hahahaha, slup slup.

1.26 a.m. Declan Nevin is cutting a small fragment off his landlady's Valium pill with a butter knife and rolling it in a slice of packet ham, which he gives to Toby and then pats his head.

Take this ta fuck, Jaysus Christ, it will shut you up, you little cunt. I've to operate on four hours' sleep because of you. As the man says, I'm shattered.

1.30 a.m. Gus Slattery has read and reread the email from Cormac Denehy several times over. In his mind he has just choked Cormac Denehy to death while Emma watched in lingerie. She then begged Gus to let him give him oral sex.

I won't be able to talk my way out of this with Father Purcell. Fuck fuck fuck. This is a complaint relating to full on blasphemy, Augustine. You'd not only be kicked out of the Society, but the college might ask you to leave the course altogether. There can't be a primary school teacher who got done for joking about defiling the corpse of Padre Pio. That's beyond the beyonds. Not a school in the twenty-six counties would have me, not even those Protestants up the North would, or the ould Catholics they have up there even, the wrong kind. I'm not letting Denehy win this. Think, Augustine. Howld on.

What if I did want to turn Padre Pio's body into a drone? No no no. Cop on now. Fuck it. OK. Wait a minute so. Let's weigh this out.

a) His body is already on display in that church over in Italy. Didn't his remains refuse to decompose or something? He's some type of Christian mummy. It was his last miracle.

b) I've seen pictures of his corpse in a glass case and people lined up beside it with Rosary beads. His remains are already worshipped.

c) It would still be the body of Padre Pio. Still venerated, still as holy as ever. It would just have the mechanised ability to fly and hover. I don't see why that is necessarily blasphemous. Why does the introduction of technology have to immediately be blasphemous?

What if I go to Purcell tomorrow and tell him that I'd been visited by Padre Pio in my sleep? And that his spirit asked me to turn his preserved corpse into a drone? I could draw up a plan, hurried scribbles that made it look divinely inspired. Sure, Noah knew fuck all about building arks when God came to him. It doesn't matter that I know nothing about making drones.

You'd maybe … OK, you'd get four smaller drones: one on each of Pio's feet and the other two for his hands. So he's splayed out, like the cat was in the YouTube video. Maybe a large propeller on his back to maintain balance. He'd have his signature brown pauper's robes on. Wait. But what if a wind came? And then Padre Pio was hovering, with his hands out, and the wind blew the robe into the blades and we lost a propeller? You couldn't have him crashing into the crowd – that would be awful. Ruin the mystery of it. You'd take the robe off then. No, you couldn't have a nude Pio. A tight-fitting body suit, like a surfer would have? Ah, feck it, no – if you don't have robes and a beard then it's not Padre Pio. I'd be codding no one with that. I'll have to design my way around the wind later. Maybe stiffen the fabric of the robe so it doesn't flutter?

I could report to Father Purcell that Padre Pio's spirit believes he could reach more people if his corpse was able to hover over crowds, doing away with the need for big queues. Fucking solar-powered and all.

d) I know for a fact that there is already a solar-powered Padre Pio statue in Italy. Paid for by the Church. As a nod towards environmentalism. This is all sounding very plausible, Augustine.

'Excuse me, Father Purcell, but last night I was visited by the spirit of Padre Pio. His hands were stained with blood. He asked me to turn his corpse into a solar-powered drone.' That could work. What's Father Purcell going to do? Say I'm lying? He couldn't – he'd have to take me at my word.

Maybe I'm not actually making this up and tonight was all orchestrated by Pio's ghost? The Lord moves in very mysterious ways. This could be divine inspiration, or maybe not – who am I to question it? Yes. *Yes.* I'd get Father Purcell to ask the college to fund a trip over to Italy for me to build Padre Pio's corpse into a drone. And I'd have Emma as my loving assistant. And I'd have her to myself, no Denehy. Check-fucking-mate, you streaky Longford cuck. They'll make a Netflix film about it, and Zac Efron will play me, and Saoirse Ronan will play Emma, and Denehy will be played by someone no one knows with spots and a huge forehead, and he'll have to watch it and apologise to me, and I won't accept the apology.

1.30 a.m. Declan Nevin is very concerned in the old kitchen below in Nicholas Street. Toby is unresponsive from the Valium. His slow, laboured breaths become shorter until they stop. He dies peacefully.

Toby? Toby? C'mon, boy. We go walkies? Would you like a biscuit? Toby? Oh fuck, oh fuck. How will I explain this to her? She'll know I was involved somehow. Dogs don't just die in the kitchen. She'll miss the fucking Valium pill. Oh my Christ, what if Lasma heard I killed a dog? She loves dogs. How could I get her back if I POISONED A DOG WITH VALIUM? FUCK FUCK FUCK FUCK FUCK …

1.30 a.m. Gus Slattery is now halfway down Nicholas Street. He is feeling very confident.

What if the drone sprays blood all over the worshippers from the corpse's hands – to give the real genuine stigmata experience? You could hide tanks of blood under Padre Pio's robes with a propellant of some sort. Then nozzles under the skin on his palms where the wounds are. And when the crowds of worshippers are on their knees, Padre Pio would hover over them and spray blood all over their faces and into their mouths, and they'd drink the holy blood. It could even be wine, and you could say the blood transubstantiated when it left the wounds. Of course. *Yes*, Augustine.

1.31 a.m. Declan Nevin is in a panic. He is holding Toby's dead body after a failed attempt to resuscitate him with a glass of water. Toby is wet now.

Oh, bollocks. How can this be happening? What if I put him out on the road? The landlady will think a car hit him. I'll say she left the doors open and he got out and was hit by a car. She'd believe that. It's a horrible thing to do to her, but as the man says, I've to be 'macky velly ann' about this. There's far more important things at stake. But he'd need a wound, though. Maybe I should hit his face a bit with the toaster? No, I can't do that. The attic window. I'll fuck him out the attic window, and when he hits the ground he'll splatter and it will look like a car did it. Yes.

1.43 a.m. Toby is dead. There is no dog heaven. His limp corpse is in the fat, worried arms of Declan Nevin. He is thrown out the attic window. His body spins in the black moonlight of Nicholas Street and hurries downwards.

1.43 a.m. Gus Slattery is consumed by the concept of turning Padre Pio's corpse into a drone and does not notice the Jack Russell terrier falling towards him from above. It impacts his left arm with great force.

Owwww, owwwww, owwwwwwwww, owwww.

1.44 a.m. Gus Slattery has spent forty-six seconds in silent panic, holding his left arm. His face is sweaty and freezing; his breaths are manic. His shoulder is bent in a way that shoulders shouldn't bend. He stares at the dead Jack Russell on the cobbles, and

stares up at the sky, and stares at the dead Jack Russell on the
cobbles, and stares up at the sky.

It can't be. Is this a sign from the Lord? Does this mean the
idea for the Padre Pio drone was real? It was the Lord working
through me? But what if it's a warning? A punishment? To not
go ahead with the drone? Nooo, no. If the Lord made Padre
Pio bleed from his wrists, feet and sides every day of his life,
then maybe he wants to hit me with dogs from the sky. To be in
communion with his suffering in his last days up on the cross.
What if I'm to be hit with a falling dog each day and that's my
penance for my divine gift? Why a dog? Of course. This started
with the cat-drone video. And dogs are pets like cats. Oh Jaysus,
he's clever alright. This is fucking sore. Maybe if I try to push
the shoulder in? Oh no, oh no, oh no. That's a new pain – I felt
that in my hole. I should probably take the dog, shouldn't I? I
mean, it could be divine. It's a relic now, isn't it? Fuck, does that
make me a saint? Owwwwwwwwwwww.

1.58 a.m. Declan Nevin is awake, looking at his ex-wife's
Facebook profile. She posted a photograph of a croissant and a
cappuccino from a café earlier in the day. There is no evidence
of a second cup across from her. Declan feels a slight reassuring
warmth in his heart, as this means that she was on her own.
However, he is unable to sleep because he just poisoned his
landlady's dog and threw the corpse out the attic window.

2.10 a.m. Gus Slattery is wandering Limerick in a daze, holding
his left arm, unable to fully process the pain due to the intensity
of his thoughts. In his right hand is Toby's leg, held like a dead

rabbit, his little limp body dangling below. Gus is frightened. He feels chosen but does not feel worthy of such a call. His phone beeps – it is a text from Emma. He rests Toby's body on his shoulder with as much ceremonial reverence as he can achieve with one hand. The dog slumps over his back. Gus is cautious not to drop the holy Toby on the ground, and imagines himself as Joseph carefully removing the dead Christ from the crucifix. Gus opens his phone with his uninjured hand and reads Emma's text.

Emma: Hey, Augustine. Look, I just want to make sure you're OK. I don't know what's going on with you and Cormac, but ye should talk to each other. If that's alright, I'd like ye both to sort it out and give me some space. Tonight was the first night I've properly spoken to either of you, and it just felt a bit off. You're probably asleep, but I'm texting at this hour because it was keeping me awake, and I just want to name it now so it's not a problem going forward in the Society. OK?

Gus: Hey, Emma. Look. Forget about that. Something really incredible just happened to me. And it's no surprise you just texted me now either. It's clearly a sign. I need to show you something. There's no time to fully explain what it is. But when you see it, you'll know how big this whole thing is. I'm going to call over to your place now. You're living on O'Connell Street, yes? 43? With the ivy on the front? x

Emma: Please, please don't do that, Augustine.

Sonic the hedgehog
Got undetectable chlamydia in Portugal
PLEASE LIKE
AND SHARE

'THE SKIN METHOD', OR GABRIEL BYRNE AS A METAMODERN WEAPON OF SOCIAL CHAOS

'I turned forty-three in April, but I have the same heart, liver and cock I had when I was twenty-three. I feel great. I don't need a doctor to test me. Big Gaybo energy. I just know it's the case, I can feel it.' – @Proudskinner8765
(translated from Ukrainian)

'I'm Benicio del Toro, I'm a big boy and I would like the kneecaps and shins of a nine-year-old, so I can run to the shop and get ice creams and then do a big poo in the toilet and tell Mam.' – Benicio del Toro?

ABSTRACT

On 6 December 2001 a video surfaced on the deep web forum Onion Party, uploaded by a user named 'Norkav'. The video appears to depict Irish actor Gabriel Byrne engaged in a conversation with Puerto Rican actor Benicio del Toro. The footage is presented as a clandestine recording. Byrne and del Toro speak to each other for six minutes and forty-two seconds. The video was initially uploaded with the title 'The Skin Method', due to Byrne's consistent use of this phrase throughout. The footage appeared on the surface web in 2011, on the Romanian website stiri Mondene, with added subtitles in Romanian, Albanian and Ukrainian. A non-subtitled version appeared on the English-language forum Reddit later that month.

The subject matter of the video created intense discussion on deep web message boards throughout the 2000s. Initially, some users posited a sceptical critique as to the authenticity of the footage. However, a divergent collective of users emerged who argued that the footage was not only genuine, but was also irrefutable evidence of a type of hidden or dark knowledge possessed only by the wealthy, powerful and famous.

This interpretation garnered a mostly male online following, first with internet users in Balkan countries and former Soviet states. This assemblage became known as the 'skinning community'; the adherents identify as 'skinners'. They began to physically practise the 'skin method' and post their results online. They would encourage others to do similar and aggressively shame those who did not. The practice of 'skinning' or using the skin method is now widespread, primarily amongst straight men in countries with broadband internet access. It operates as a religious or spiritual practice, but without any central organisation or doctrine. This has created a global public health crisis and is fuelling human rights abuses.

This text will discuss the original 2001 upload, known in online skinning communities as the 'Norkav Cut' or '642'. Both Gabriel Byrne and Benicio del Toro, who are depicted in the video, have refused, consistently, to comment on or acknowledge the footage. This text will further the proposition that the 'Skin Method' video is a hoax.

VISUAL ANALYSIS: TOWARDS A CONTEXT

The footage opens on a darkened space. Two figures sit across from each other, and between them is a small table. The figures are both in silhouette. There is no atmospheric sound from the space itself, only a faint high-pitched emission, accompanied by a lower droning white-noise hum. Both noises are conducive with the sound output of VHS camcorders.

At twelve seconds, a cacophony of movement can be heard. The screen flashes with an intense white glow. The lens adjusts to the change in light. We see that figure one, who was sitting on the left, has just retracted a small curtain and let some sunlight into the space. Figure two remains in situ. It becomes visibly clear that the room is a mobile home or caravan. To the far left is a kitchenette with wooden fixtures; to the right of that, a rounded swing door, typically present in mobile accommodation.

Through comparative analysis of mobile homes and caravans, the model has been identified. The specific shape of the window and an illumination on the table that indicates the presence of a skylight suggests that the vehicle is a Winnebago Vectra class motor home, model 194RV.

On the extreme right of the screen is a blurred object, yellow or dark brown in colour. This detail has led some in the skinning community to believe that the camcorder is hidden in a bowl of fruit and that the blur is caused by the edge of an orange or, as posited by Reddit user 'SkinmanHunk', an over-ripe nectarine that is partially obstructing the camera lens. Del Toro also makes reference to a fig during his conversation with Byrne, which adds substance to this claim.

Figure one returns to his seat. It is a man. He is now physically closer to the camera. Facial analysis of the video using the open-source software FaceScanner has confirmed, with a two per cent margin of error, that figure one is Irish actor Gabriel Byrne. Byrne is wearing a teal shirt, unbuttoned at the collar; on his shoulders is a cream-coloured floor-length coat.

Figure two sits across from Byrne. Only the back of his head and shoulders are visible. He wears a scarlet silk shirt. Cross analysis with the 1995 film *The Usual Suspects* would strongly suggest that figure two is the actor Benicio del Toro. Further, it is now widely believed that 'The Skin Method' was clandestinely filmed in 1994 on the film set of *The Usual Suspects*, San Pedro, California; that the interior location seen in the video is Gabriel Byrne's actor's trailer; and that Byrne and del Toro are in costume as *Usual Suspects* characters Dean Keaton and Fred Fenster respectively.

TRANSCRIPTION OF THE PRIMARY SOURCE: RECLAIMING SINCERITY IN A POST-TRUTH DIALOGIC?

Note: the first instance of dialogue occurs at 00:36. Both parties are denoted by their respective initials in this transcription.

On the surface of the oval table situated between Byrne and del Toro are four small plastic bags that contain a white substance. There is also what appears to be a razor blade beside the bags.

BDT: May I have one of those figs?

GB: No, look here, look down at these.

BDT: I've noticed those. I don't do cocaine, Gabriel. I'd actually rather not even be around it.

GB: But you said you wanted to go over a few lines, wha? Hahahahah.

BDT: Very funny. Big clever Gabriel. Look, if you'd like to go over the script, just you and I, here, we can do that. If that's not why you asked me here, I'd prefer to go to my own trailer and chill.

GB: It's not coke, Benny, yiz fucking dope. It's the skin method.

BDT: It is very clearly cocaine.

GB: It's not. Lookah.

01:13 Byrne uses the index finger of his left hand to point at the four bags on the table, beginning from his left and moving to the right. His demeanour is calm.

GB: That's me when I'm nine. That's me when I'm eleven. That's me when I'm eighteen. That's me when I'm twenty-one.

BDT: I don't follow you, Gabriel.

GB: It's bags of me skin. I've been collecting me skin.

BDT: You're asking me to snort your skin?

GB: Do you own a computer?

BDT: No, I don't own a computer. Are we here because you want me to snort your skin that you've saved in bags?

GB: I have a computer. I've had computers for donkey's years.

BDT: Is this real life? Is this a real conversation that's happening in real life?

GB: Why don't you like computers?

BDT: I didn't say I didn't like computers.

GB: Computers are always getting viruses or things are going wrong with them. It's a machine, but a machine that can get sick. They're fascinating.

Byrne slams his fist on the table enthusiastically. This noise triggers the camcorder's internal audio compression, causing a dip in audio that distorts Byrne's words. It has been posited that 'Fucking marvellous' or 'Jaysus, fucking marvellous' are the words uttered at this point.

GB: So you create these things called system restore points, right – it's like a memory of when the computer is healthy. So when the computer gets sick, or is working wrong, you just reboot it to the last time it was healthy. You restore the system to a previous point. Everything is perfect again. It's bleedin' incredible.

BDT: That is interesting, I'll admit that. Why do you have four bags of your skin? And are you asking me to snort your skin?

GB: These are my system restore points.

BDT: Bullshit.

GB: Nope. These bags contain earlier versions of me.

BDT: ...

GB: This is the skin method. You see, every day our bodies shed skin.

BDT: Like snakes? I saw a snake doing that at a reptile enclosure in the zoo.

GB: Yes. But snakes, they shed it all in one go. We shed little bits. We lose tiny bits of ourselves – it just falls off as skin and dust or whatever. All the time. Literally, the physical person you are here, now, is a different body of matter to the person you were six months ago. That person is gone. Your skin, your organs. Everything has shed and regenerated. Even though you feel like you, you're not really you. Benicio six months ago was a different cluster of cells. He's dead. He might as well be someone else.

BDT: Holy moly, how did I never think of it like this?

GB: I know … We die and are reborn all the time. We're simultaneously dying and being reborn right now. And do you know how you grow back?

BDT: I do not.

GB: DNA – your DNA is like a blueprint for Benicio. When you shed a bit of skin, your DNA tells that skin to grow back. And it does this to all the cells in your body. And this is why your cells grow back into Benicio del Toro but don't grow back as another person. The DNA won't allow that. It's your body's instruction manual. And it was written when your parents rode each other. Your instruction manual is like a mixture of their instruction manuals. But the pages on this manual get faded as time passes, and information gets lost. That's how ageing happens. Your DNA changes, so what grows back is still Benicio del Toro, but it's an older one.

BDT: I've always wondered how that works. Like, how do I grow and get old and stuff? Like, I can't see it happening, but then I look at, maybe, a movie I did, and I can see that I'm older now. I've always wondered how it happened.

GB: Ya, exactly. These bags contain earlier versions of me, of Gabriel Byrne. So I save my skin. I choose a night, and I run up and down my body with a shoehorn, or a bit of a plastic cup, and I scrape off as many skin cells as possible into a bag to collect my DNA as it is in that moment. Been doing it since I was a child. I turned forty-four in May, but I have the same heart, liver and cock I had when I was twenty-four. I feel great. I don't need a doctor to test me. Big Gaybo energy. I just know it's the case, I can feel it. Remember with the computer?

BDT: The system restore points?

GB: So I have these system restore points here in these bags. But they don't just work on me. Have you any physical complaints recently? You must be in your thirties now, are you?

BDT: Yes. My knees. I used to enjoy running, but now I cannot anymore. My knees seize up, they swell.

GB: I'd a whopper set of knees on me when I was nine. The neighbours had an Alsatian, and I'd race him to the shops. Here, do a line of nine-year-old me. Sort it right out. You just have to think about your knees and imagine being me as a child.

Del Toro picks up one of the bags, and holds it towards the light.

BDT: So, is it just your skin in here? It looks very powdery to just be a person's skin?

GB: Ya, I'll rack out a line here. Have a go. And repeat this line: 'I'm Benicio del Toro, I'm a big boy and I would like the kneecaps and shins of a nine-year-old, so I can run to the shop and get ice creams and then do a big poo in the toilet and tell Mam.'

Del Toro repeats this sentence and proceeds to snort a line of powder from the first bag on the left. Byrne then asks del Toro to jump on the spot and to tell him if his knees feel better. Del Toro reports back that they do, in fact, feel better. As the footage progresses, del Toro snorts more of the powder from the other bags, announcing that he wishes to grow the skin of an eleven-year-old, the liver of an eighteen-year-old and the genitals of a twenty-one-year-old. Upon each snort, del Toro loudly recites a specific memory from Byrne's life as dictated to him by Byrne. Del Toro confidently asserts to Byrne that he immediately feels younger, more energetic and more confident.

At 04:13, Byrne produces a compact mirror from his trouser pocket and hands it to del Toro. Del Toro looks in the mirror while Byrne compliments him on how young and beautiful his skin looks, referring repeatedly to del Toro's forehead as a 'nipper's arse'. Del Toro agrees with him on several occasions and seems enamoured by his own reflection. Due to the inferior quality offered by the VHS recording, it is not apparent to the viewer if there is any visible change in del Toro. Close up analysis of 05:02, where the side of del Toro's face is visible, does not yield an adequate view of his skin. Nor do any of the cursory shots of his reflection in the compact mirror. Byrne himself snorts from the bags too. At one point, he is seen rotating his shoulder cuff in a windmill motion and saying to del Toro, 'Look at that movement. That's my shoulder when I was eighteen. Do you think I'd be able to do this now? I wouldn't. Coz this isn't the same shoulder I had this morning. This is an earlier version of my shoulder from when I was eighteen. I'd knock a stallion out with this swing. Just hit him in the forehead. Out. Cold.'

The footage ends with Byrne urging del Toro not to tell anybody about the skin method, that it is a very secret method of personal rejuvenation invented by Byrne and that to leak it would mean that 'no one would die, you see – they'd all keep snorting earlier versions of themselves, and then there'd be too many people, and what would happen is that everyone's feet would fall onto the ground at once and crush the Earth, and then we'd all be floating in space scratching our bollix. So only a small few people can know about the skin method.'

BEYOND DEEPFAKES: TOWARDS AN EXPLANATION
The dialogue between Byrne and del Toro contains glaring errors. General consensus from online skin-method sceptics is that the audio is likely faked. However, the legitimacy of the footage is much harder to disprove.

With regard to the dialogue, most notably, Byrne mentions system restore points. Byrne, who was born in 1950, could not have been in possession of a personal computer throughout his childhood. It is also impossible that Byrne would mention 'system restore points' in 1994. System restore points were first introduced to the public by Microsoft in the Windows Millennium edition of the operating system in the year 2000.

There is a strong probability that Byrne and del Toro's voices were replicated by voice actors or that an early incarnation of AI voice replication technology was used. However, software analysis that would detect digital artefacts in this respect has been inconclusive.

I will now interrogate the footage and offer some possible explanation for the visuals.

A) A generally accepted explanation, though not proven, is that the footage is genuine. The Norkav Cut is a found clandestine recording of Gabriel Byrne and Benicio del Toro in San Pedro, California, on the set of *The Usual Suspects*, recorded in May 1994. It depicts the two men conversing and ingesting a powdery substance from several bags – possibly cocaine, heroin, ketamine or methamphetamine, or a combination of all four. What ensues is both men behaving strangely while under the influence of the narcotic. However, the actual conversation that took place remains unknown, and establishing it through lip reading is impossible due to the low quality of the footage and poor lighting.

B) The footage is genuine. It depicts both actors engaged in professional discourse – possibly rehearsing a scene from *The Usual Suspects* that never made it to the final version or engaging in method acting by staying grounded within the characters of Dean Keaton and Fred Fenster, taking stage cocaine (usually glucose) and behaving erratically to enhance their on-screen performances.

C) The footage is entirely fake. Deepfake technology or even prosthetics were used to create false versions of Gabriel Byrne and Benicio del Toro as a hoax.

THE DOPPELGÄNGER AND METAMODERN PROBLEMATICS IN
ONLINE CULTURE: WHO WOULD DO THIS AND WHY?

Within months of the Norkav Cut emerging in 2001, isolated
incidents of real-life skin-method practice amongst young men
began to appear in Armenia, Moldova, Ukraine and Georgia. An
article appeared in the Ukrainian newspaper *Fakty i Kommen-
tarii* on 6 January 2002 with the headline 'Kiev Thugs with
Bloodied Shins Demand the Skin of Children'. According to the
article: 'Young men who have scraped their shins raw and were
seen acting boisterously yesterday caused chaos in the region of
Lipinka. [...] The thugs walked door to door, swinging hammers
and demanding that residents "scrape the skin of any child in
the house into these bags".'

A clear trend began to emerge in former Soviet countries inspired
by the skin-method video. Men began to believe that they
could achieve a type of eternal childhood or youthful vigour
through the use of personal system-restore points via collected
skin. While they at first began to collect their own skin from
their bodies, often to the point of skinning themselves raw, they
moved on to procuring the skin of children through threatening
or menacing behaviour. Frightened parents were left with no
choice but to scrape their children each night and leave bags of
skin outside, often on front porches or simply on the handles of
their apartment doors. These were then collected by the gangs.
Men who snorted the skin of a child would enter a frenzy of
behaviour conducive with the age of the victim's skin: throwing
tantrums, defecating themselves, gorging on available confectionary or, in the absence of confectionary, gorging on pebbles
painted like confectionary, or crying for hours in loud bawls. A

dysfunctional social phenomenon had emerged that seemed to transcend the expectations of what post-Soviet society would deem acceptable behaviour for adult men.

'GABRIEL DOES NOT LIE': THE TRUSTWORTHINESS OF GABRIEL BYRNE'S FACE

This practice began to operate in a quasi-religious fashion, with skinners explaining their behaviour by presenting 'The Skin Method' as a truthful document. Attempts to explain to skinners that the video of Byrne and del Toro may have been faked were met with hostility. Followers of skinning who had grown up under a bombardment of Soviet propaganda did not seem to apply any criticality to the footage. It is medically impossible to reverse ageing or to enhance human DNA through the snorting of our own or another person's skin. A common online retort to this, used by followers of skinning, translates to 'Gabriel does not lie'.

To fully contextualise this, one must interrogate the role of Gabriel Byrne's early film output and its importance in 1980's Soviet society, in particular male culture. *Excalibur* (1981), *Gothic* (1986) and *Lionheart* (1987) were hugely popular in the Soviet states as widely traded black-market videos. However, the distinction between Gabriel Byrne the actor and the hyperreal icon of Byrne began to radically separate in Soviet culture. Gabriel Byrne became a type of folk saint, with a large mural of him being painted in the Donetsk region of Ukraine in the early '90s. Further murals emerged in Romania, Uzbekistan and Georgia. These murals were not sanctioned by the state but instead were painted by ordinary people as an alternative to the state-sanctioned Soviet imagery of control that was ubiquitous towards the collapse of the Soviet Union. Whenever these murals were painted over by police, men would move Gabriel Byrne iconography into the privacy of their homes.

The graduation of Gabriel Byrne from Hollywood actor to folk saint in late Soviet society can be attributed to his facial features. Byrne, while Irish, possesses a cranial profile and facial musculature that is archetypically and idealistically Slavic. His forehead is dominant, his cheekbones are high and his nose is definite and strong on his face. His profile became unconsciously fetishised within Soviet culture as that of a loving, benevolent alpha male. In contrast to actual leaders like Vyacheslav Molotov, Nikolai Podgorny or Dmitry Ustinov, who became associated with untrustworthiness, Byrne became the unlikely face of trust and truth.

CONCLUSION: THE WEAPONISATION OF GABRIEL BYRNE'S HEAD
AS ASYMMETRICAL WARFARE

It is the conclusion of this text that 'The Skin Method' video is a hoax. While uncertainty remains around the footage itself, the audio elements are most definitely faked. What is real is the devastating impact that the video has had on society since its emergence eighteen years ago. The practice of saving and snorting one's own skin and, more troublingly, the snorting of the skin of children has developed into a black-market industry with global child exploitation at its core. With Romania likely to elect its first skinner leader, Tudorel Ponta, a man who proudly exhibits extensive scabbing on his legs and snorts skin directly from the bodies of constituents' children at rallies, it is clear that the footage has contributed towards an aggressive destabilisation of society in former Soviet states, with dangerously unpredictable geopolitical challenges ahead.

There is growing evidence that 'The Skin Method' was created by the Russian FSB some time in 2001. A knowing hoax, which traded upon Gabriel Byrne's status as a folk saint who represented truth and reliability to young men in Eastern Europe, it was released at a time of crisis and deliberately targeted young men – men who were old enough to remember their childhoods under communism but grew into adolescence after the collapse of the union, a time of social, cultural and political limbo. These men have been manipulated into believing that they can live in a state of eternal or enhanced youth through a never-ending search for system restore points. This is increasingly leading to democracies that no longer function as democracies, due to the populace straining under the continual theatre of irrationality that plays out online, on the news and in their communities. There is no truth or reliability in a society where people try and revisit earlier versions of themselves through bags of skin.

Gabriel Byrne has been weaponised: he is being used as a deadly weapon in a battlefield of asymmetrical warfare. This investigation asks, how many more requests from world leaders will it take for Gabriel Byrne to prove on camera, or on a speaking tour, that snorting his own skin has no effect? Did Byrne act with Russia? Who recorded the initial footage and why? Will Byrne publicly act to debunk 'The Skin Method'? And in a post-truth society, would it even work?

DARN SUBMERGED

wanted to ask the man with the moustache behind the counter if he thought there were too many gerbils in the cage or if they ever felt pure frightened from being so near the python's tank. Is the python deaf from being albino and does he hiss at them, and do they think they'll get eaten? But mostly I needed to know if fourteen gerbils were happy in this one cage and it so tiny. Coz last week I went past and had a squint int'it, and there was one dead, and I swear down I must have walked past the same window another eight or nine times throughout the day and her little body was still there, looking like a sleeping chick but with the pink tail on her that hadn't grown all leathery yet, and all the other gerbils just pure walking over her. It was a scandal. There's no way they could be happy at all. So I stuck my head in the door of the pet shop and said, 'Here, do you see you, do ya? You've too many gerbils in that cage.'

And then he gets up off his seat, pure raging, and he says, 'I seen your fella with the red Adidas jacket last week, the fucking junkie, and I know it was him who took the best part of a hundred euro out of that till, and I'll bury him if I catch him. I'll murder him stone dead.'

There was all mad heat across my eyebrows from that comment, the cheek of him. 'He's not my fella,' I said. 'Barely even talks to him, I does, you gowl.' Stared him out of it then. 'Why've you so many gerbils in the one cage? It's cruel,' I says.

'Fuck 'em,' he says. And then he gets up from behind the counter and pulls out the handle of a brush from beside him and walks towards me like he's going to bate me, and he was wearing a pure manky green jumper, and it looked like sick all down the front of it, and he says, 'Fuck off out of here talking about gerbils, you whore. You're only trying to distract me so that scumbag of yours can come in and rob the till.'

So I says, 'Go'way, you'll do fuck all with your jumper full of sick, hahahaha,' and then he stops, and looks down at his jumper and, hahaha, pure big embarrassed head on him, I swear, mortified he was.

He says, 'It's not sick, that's raw eggs. I was feeding a load of hawks.'

And I says, 'Whatever, hun,' but like a Yank would say it, like, ripping the piss out of him. He looked like a prick and I walked off, letting him see how proud I was over his gammy jumper, the fucking cunt, like, pure shoving fourteen gerbils in one cage and letting them die – the guards should be down crucifying him for cruelty towards animals, state of him.

It was the bones of half two up by William Street. It was only April and lads had their tops off, showing off their abs, haha, gomies. I seen Lala sitting up against the wall of Boots, and he says, 'Any fags?'

I says, 'I'm off 'em four days – I swear they were giving me TB.'

'Ah now, Shirley girl, they're delicious, though,' he says.

So I says, 'Go'way, Lala, with your "delicious" fags, you metaller, hahaa. G'waff and listen to Linkin Park.' Felt my face go awful puce, forgot about Darn, his older brother. He was a pure metaller, and he used to listen to Linkin Park and Nirvana and all them, and Lala used listen to them too, and we'd slag him and say he was only copying Darn, and then last year Darn killed himself below'n the river. 'I'm so sorry, Lala love. I didn't mean nothing by that, calling you a metaller. I didn't mean anything about Darn, pet. I'm so sorry, my god.' Lala changed a bit when I said that. He stopped leaning back pure cool, and I could see in his eyes that there was this fear and hurt in them, and he didn't want to feel like that at this moment and was fair scarlet that I could see that on him.

He put his left hand up t'is mouth and bit at the top parts of his fingers and says, 'I know you didn't mean that, Shirley, don't be worrying, beure. It's hard, like, that's all I can say. It's hard. I can't properly feel that he's gone, even though I know he's gone. I forget he's dead, and then I remember he is and it feels like when I first heard the news.'

My head didn't know how to react to that at all, pure scared that if I said anything more he'd start bawling, and then the boys with the no-tops would see and he'd be mortified in front of them, so I just gave him a bit of a hug. I felt like kissing the forehead off him too, but didn't want to go that far in case he thought I fancied him, and I says, 'That cunt with the moustache above below in Scampy's pet shop was saying you robbed out his till.'

'Fuck him, he's a spoofer,' says Lala.

'I swear down if he doesn't start minding them gerbils I'll break him. I'll burn him inside in his bed, I swear on the holy picture, cuz will get bleeded,' I says.

'Hahahaa, Shirley girl, go'way and buy yourself a few gerbils, kid,' he says.

'I've no room,' I says.

'Have you a few euro?' he says. So I gave him two fifty-five coz it's all I had in my pocket, and he went up away towards all the lads with their tops off. Darn was fierce good to Lala. He'd be minding him, like. Watching out for him, keeping off the no-top snakes who do be preying on young feens with their upjohns. Getting them all ready for oxys and then brown. Lala had the lost look on him since Darn died.

I was mad hanging for fags. There was a pure grandad smoking Major beside the bus stop and the aroma was divine, and Major are rotten, now, but it was beautiful, that second-hand smell that's nicer than smoking the actual fag itself, and I nearly went over to him. Thinking in my head what I'd say, using different words and questions over in my mind. 'Excuse me, sir, can I have one of your cigarettes, please? I left mine at home,' and I could see him giving me one and all. But I knew fucking full well what'd happen. I'd take two long pulls, and it'd feel class for about a second, and then pure rotten, and I'd remember the sore throat I had last month where I couldn't swallow, and I'd feel like a waster. The last four days of being off 'em would be for nothing, and I'd have to start all over, so I walked the opposite direction, down to the bottom of O'Connell Street, near Debenhams.

I was itching in my mind – I'd get a tingle that'd make my body shiver, and I knew the only way to stop it was a pull off a fag. I wanted to dig the head off myself – like, I was annoyed with my own body for craving them. My own fag habit wasn't too bad, about eight Marlboro a day, or maybe a few more if there was a pouch of tobacco around the place. You don't think you're addicted until you try to stop, and then that's how you know. And I'd say to myself, it's only fags, Shirley. It's not like Lala and the boys with the upjohns – you'd see them looking white and ready to cry. Heads on them like they're watching cunts get melted under a bus and can't look away from it. I'd have an odd upjohn pill myself, now, especially if I feel a panic. It will just stop the feeling and I can pure chill out, without worry driving me stone mad. But I'd control it.

Now though, my stomach had a wicked ould knot inside in it, that acid pain, like, where it'll climb up and burn the throat out of you, and I could listen to it rising from my hole. I gaped up and seent the lads with no tops skulling Dutch and throwing shapes, lamping sideways for hassle with the bowzy gatches on them. They'd hide their bleeders inside in dustbins and pull 'em out if any ould telpis with a big innocent head came looking for upjohns or brown and still hadn't paid over their whack on tick. So I went into McDonald's for a baby strawberry milkshake, and I said a prayer for the cold milk of it sliding down inside in me and putting out my fire. There's a sour rain that walks in off the river when there's hassle in Limerick – you taste it with your feet.

I'd thirty-five euro above in my account, and I fucking knew if I didn't do something soon fifteen of that would be gone on twenty Marlboro by the day's end. There's a shop up by Roches Street and it sells them electric fags. My nana does be pure pulling on hers since the emphysema, and I never seen her near fags no more, like. So I heads in. It was ten euro and looked like a silver biro. 'Do you know about the coil?' your man behind the counter says.

'I don't, no,' I says, so he shows me how you open up the top, and pour in the liquid so it soaks in for a minute before you take a pull. There was all loads of different small bottles full of the vape fluid, all different flavours like a sweetshop, one that said it tasted like Fanta and another that said it tasted like mint ice cream.

'How many cigarettes did you smoke a day?' he asked me.

'About four,' I said.

'We'll start you off on the 6 mg of nicotine then.'

So I walked out and headed up off towards the top of O'Connell Street, with the electric fag inside in my hand. I looked a bit like a gomey, now, to tell you the truth, pure showing off and posing with my electric fag, so I kind of half-hid it in my palm so my fingers covered it, like you'd do with a pinner. And I took a drag, and it tasted like peach air freshener, and it was almost harsh, like – it wasn't really that nice. But I felt it at the back of my throat – it was faint, not the power of a fag, but it was there, that junior sting, and it crawled all down my body and back up into my head, and it tore at the craving. The part of me that wanted a fag, it was calming it. So I took another pull, a strong one, so strong that the top of the vape got dead hot in my palm and I was afraid it'd explode and blow the fingers off me, hahaha. And this time, I felt the sting in my chest. My god, yes, orgasmic, will you stop, this is fucking divine, go'way beure. When I blew out, this big cloud came out of my mouth. It wasn't smoke, more like steam off the top of a kettle. It didn't fly up and off like fag smoke; it hung a bit, like it was pure heavier than smoke.

I was thrilled with myself, sitting down on the bench in the People's Park watching a dog sniffing a dandelion. What would she want with a dandelion, like? Pure diva, fucking Mariah Carey over, hahaha. And I was dragging into the electric fag – I swear to god, I was ateing it. And I wasn't thinking about real fags at all. The idea of them was rotten even. Leaving a big taste in my mouth and feeling manky after you'd smoke it, with the smell of it all over me and I'd get a bang of it any time a wind blew my hair into my face. Go'way. At least now I'd smell like peach air freshener, and there were people walking past, and I could see that they were wondering where the lovely smell was coming from, and I'd say to myself, 'It's coming off me, hun, walk on,' coz a few of 'em were staring at me a bit, like.

After a while I noticed that every time I took a drag off it, there was this sort of whistle sound. It wasn't loud – it was like if you pulled a mug across a glass table – but it was a small bit annoying. Then, the more I'd take pulls, the more I'd only pay attention to the whistling noise, and it'd be louder. But I couldn't tell if it was actually getting louder or if I just thought it was louder coz I was paying it too much attention. So I walked away out of the park, up over towards a bit of traffic and a few voices, like, so I wouldn't be hearing it the whole time.

It was when I reached as far as the monument up by the Crescent that I started to get a bit freaked out. It was around seven o'clock, coz the traffic was getting heavy heading out of town towards Dooradoyle, and I was pissed off with myself for not wearing a jacket – you can't trust April, cuz. And there was clouds too, but the real high ones that are so bright you'd get dizzy if you looked up at them. The whistly noise out of the electric fag was starting to get so loud that I nearly wanted to stop pulling off it altogether. Pure *meeep, meeep. Meeep meeeeeeeeeep, meeeeeeeeeeeeeep*. The noise was bringing a migraine on top of me. I'd drag out of it, and then the sound would hurt my ears and it'd feel like ice across my eyebrows. I wasn't right at all. So I sat down on one of them huge steps in front of a solicitor's office, trying to settle my head, and I looked off in the distance towards a wheelie bin, and I swear, I just seen this little brown flash behind the bin, like a bird or a rat. But then it came out, and it wasn't no bird or rat. It was one of the gerbils from the pet shop. Just wandering around town, like, not a bother on her. Fair fucks, hun – I thought it was gas, like. That gowl with the moustache and his puke jumper up above in Scampy's pet shop probably tried to open the cage at the end of the day, and then one probably jumped out coz he's stuffing them all into that tiny space – serves him right. Then I got worried coz, like, a rat or a mouse, they know what they're doing. They've holes or whatever that they live in. But this gerbil doesn't know nothing about Limerick – they're from a cage. I walked over towards the bin, crouched down, pure slow, sneaking, like, to catch her. Nosy cunts in traffic gaping at me. Mind your business, Donal, I'm rescuing a gerbil. I could see the little furry yellow back on her as I got close, and then she ran away down the back of a bridal store, so I went after her.

At the back of the bridal store, there was the mad strong smells of men's piss and nettles growing sideways from the walls. And a dog's shit. My feet scrunched on empty blister packets from upjohns over the ground. Seeing that made me want one. I seen the gerbil over in the corner, under a window, beside a drain, like she was drinking out of it. I moved forward more a few steps and then seen another wan, up on a big metal air-conditioner yoke – he was gaping down at me with the pure small black eyes. And he wouldn't stop glancing. Pure staring right through me, poking in and out of me with his eyes – it didn't feel nice at all. And so I says, 'Fuck off, you, gerbil. Why you staring at me? I was only inside in the pet shop today, fighting for you.' And the gerbil did nothing – he just kept gazing from up above on the big square grey air-conditioner box. So then I gets the fuck out of the alley, coz I didn't feel safe at all.

I walked away back down O'Connell Street fast, nervous, so I took big pulls out of the electric fag, and the whistle sound, it wasn't just a whistle no more – it was like a song. It sounded like Avicii, like you'd pure buzz off the song if you heard it on yips. That freaked me out, so I took another pull off it to check if I wasn't gone wired to the moon, and sure enough, the electric fag was making a tune. I turnt around and there was about five of them gerbils from the pet shop, just walking behind me, following. And I says, 'Here. Would ye fuck off and leave me alone. I'm on yere side. Did ye not see me earlier? I was the only one asking about yere cage. Why are ye coming after me?' And the gerbils said nothing, they just kept staring, looking through me. I felt filthy, I wanted to shower, I felt hurt. The acid in my stomach came up through my throat and into my mouth. I spat it down onto the ground and didn't want to look at the colour of it.

I fucking bounded, I ran, to get away from them gerbils. But they were at my heels. I knocked an ould man down, pushed through him. I wanted to stop and say sorry to him, but if I did that the gerbils would catch up. I found myself in traffic – it was at a standstill, not moving, like, but I was in the middle of the road and they were all beeping horns. Mad red face on me and hot, overwhelmed. Them gerbils were all hiding under the car wheels, just staring at me. 'Will ye fucking help me?' I says to the drivers. 'Fucking stop them, will ye?' One blonde-haired bitch in a car rolled up her window and pretended she didn't see me. I wanted to kill her. My heart was a balloon about to burst.

I seent the front door of the Augustinians' church, and I remembered my nana saying that if anyone ever came after you that you can go into a church and claim sanitary, and then they can't touch you, even if it's the guards. So I fucking legged it, up in the door. Pure old church just standing there in the middle of Limerick city, like. There wasn't no one doing Mass or nothing, just one or two people saying their own prayers in the quiet. I'd gotten up as far as the top seats, and I didn't want to distract anyone from their prayers – I was trying to be as quiet as I could. I was just pure staring at the altar ahead of me, like I was walking up for communion, coz if I looked back and seen one gerbil, I'd scream the head off myself. There was the big stained-glass window above the altar, all purple and orange, and me man was holding a yellow apple with a cross on it, except there wasn't no sun coming in, it was the streetlight from the alley outside, and that looked gammy. I sat down. The quietness inside in the church had me feeling less scared, and it wasn't like out in the road with all the cunts in their cars staring me out of it and beeping. I was nearly ready to chill out when I looked up, and there up on the altar was a gerbil. Brown and rude, like I was nothing, like I didn't matter. Just sitting there, up on the altar, staring at me, making me feel filthy. And there was this stabbing pain in my chest, like pure ashamed I was, and I wanted to roar out every cry I'd ever had, all at once, in one go. 'Can ye fucking see him? Why are ye just letting him do that? Why won't ye do anything? Look at what he's doing to me?' I started roaring. And the few people saying prayers to themselves got up off their seats and ignored me – they walked away. I saw more. Up on pillars, under seats, on top of the confession boxes. Fucking gerbils. Everywhere. And I'd had enough, and I was angry with all them pricks walking off. Like, they're supposed to be the Catholics, and they're just ignoring me and letting them gerbils do what they want. So I seen this statue, it was a Child of Prague, and I grabbed him by his legs and started roaring, screaming 'Sanitary, sanitary' at the gerbils. And I started bateing the statue off the tiles on the floor, breaking bits of plaster off him and all, as a warning to them gerbils that I didn't want to hurt them – if they go away, they can, like, but if they come near me, I'll lash the faces off them with this Child of Prague. Then the fucking guards came and dragged me out, and one bean garda had me by the hair. They didn't arrest me or nothing, just fucked me off out of the church. It wasn't warm no more, just an April night with sour rain on the way. The boys were at the bottom of William Street now with their tops back on, and I could see Lala looking for upjohns off them. My tongue was hanging out for one too.

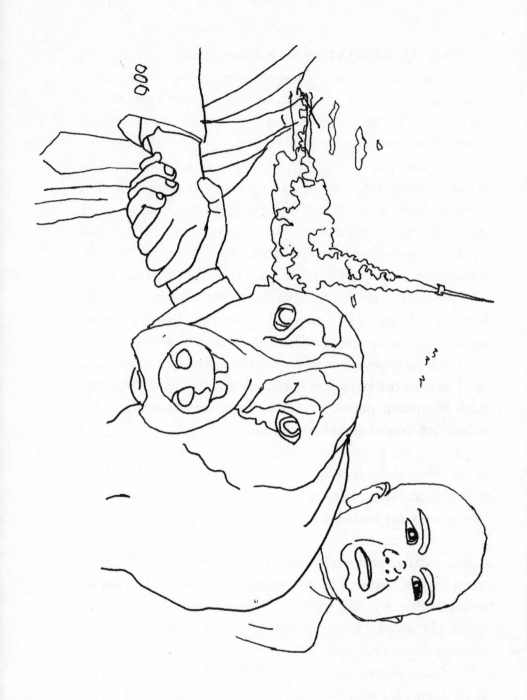

CHRISTOPHER WALKING

Jack Foley never got to go to college after the Leaving Cert like the rest of us. He doesn't speak like you or me. When his mouth opens, it makes noises. The noises are like words, but they're not words. So if you meet Jack, he prefers to use text on his phone instead of speaking. When you see Jack in the pub with his friends, they are all logged into a WhatsApp group, not talking out loud, but still having the craic, drinking pints, sheepishly looking over at Sophie Cadogan and them ones across by the fag machine. But all of the lads in Jack's gang are communicating with each other in a group text. All night, even when they're shitfaced by the seventh pint, they're looking up at each other, wincing smiles or grimaces at what's just been typed, like it's all a big private joke, with their chequered shirts honking of the same spicy Paco Rabanne aftershave.

This is all just so that Jack can be included in their fun. It's to be admired, I suppose. Other lads might not invite him out and just go drinking without him. They really put in that effort to include him. It is kind of sweet that they can carry on their friendship like that. It's not pleasant for me, though. I can't stand it. I can't be in the same pub as them because it hurts me. I feel it as a little hateful lump at the back of my stomach. Worse still, there's only two pubs, and their pub is the good pub. Jack wasn't always this way. He was like the rest of us. Jack was also my friend, and his friends were my friends too. This is not the case anymore. Here's the reason why.

There's a part in the film *The Deer Hunter* where the actor Christopher Walken is forced to play a game of Russian roulette. You know the game, you've seen it. A single bullet is placed in a revolver and the chamber is spun. You then put the gun to your temple, and there is a one out of six chance that you'll blow the head off yourself when the trigger is pulled. Christopher Walken was the one in six. He blew the head off himself. Kind of. He was wearing this red bandana and you could tell that there was a little pump in amongst the folds of fabric that squirted out blood when the gun went off. If you looked at the left side of the bandana, it had this unnecessary bulge that looked really out of place. It's where the blood squib was hidden. I suppose in the seventies, when it came out, people watching it in the cinema didn't see this or care. You'd hardly ask the projectionist to rewind a scene if you were in the cinema, like. But anyway, I see it. So there wasn't any brains. Just a stupid looking spurt of blood that ruins the scene a bit.

We didn't have guns where I grew up. A farmer might have had a shotgun, but there was no way we were getting our hands on a revolver. Handguns are long banned in Ireland. I asked my da – he's a guard. 'There's no handguns, only illegal ones,' he said. But the lads and I, we'd watch that *Deer Hunter* scene an awful lot on YouTube because it spoke to the divil in us. The terror of it. I'm not into the guns of it, or the violence of it, or the pain of it. It's the risk of it, I suppose. It cut through the boredom, and we all wanted to be Christopher Walken in that scene.

It's embarrassing to say it now, but we kind of had this desire to blow the heads off ourselves. Not a suicidal thing – just the thrill of it, and to be remembered for doing it, I suppose. I dunno. To be called a mad bastard. Ridiculous teenage carry-on.

We'd hang around in Teddy's shed at the back of his family's farm. It was just an old purple Bell shipping container, corrugated on the outside, with a bit of carpet thrown down and a yellow couch with worn springs that made it extra soft to sit on. On weekends we could drink cans there. The space was ours, except for a small bit at the back where Teddy's da kept tools on a bench. There were nails, drill bits and a claw hammer that left your hands smelling like rust. A piece of the handle had been chewed off by Teddy's dead St Bernard. The shed was fairly massive – thinking back, you'd be happy to get an apartment like it up in Dublin now. It kept the rain off you, and we had somewhere to smoke rollies after school. It was grand. You'd drag cow shit in and it wouldn't even matter. And we wanted more than anything to play Russian roulette below there.

'Where could we get a gun? Could we make one ourselves out of a pipe?'

'Can't you buy guns on the dark web?'

'Bullets are easy to get, but guns are hard to get.'

'You could find instructions online and make one in the metalwork lab in school?'

'Watch this video, it's of old men in Karachi who copy guns and bate them out of old tin rooves. If they can do it, we can.'

This was the patter every day after school. Half-joking, half-serious, making rollies out of spent fag butts from the last Saturday's can sesh. But it was Booly who first suggested that we might not need a gun at all. There was a second way to play Russian roulette, he said, if we as a group, collectively, became the gun. So that's what we did.

Teddy's da had a small carousel for feeding sheep, and we brought this into the shed one Tuesday. It was heavy and awkward. It looked like something you'd see in a playground. Imagine a really small carnival carousel, but without the little plastic horses on it. A circular platform, about eight feet in diameter, with six dividers and a small trough in each, and it could be spun easily. Its intended purpose was to keep the sheep moving so their feet wouldn't get stuck in wet mud. Kept them trotting in a circle while they ate. But a human, a very bored human, or up to six bored humans could also sit their arses on one of the little troughs and use it a bit like a merry-go-round if they had a friend who'd spin it for them.

There were seven of us in total. We were all in the same class in sixth year in a small school out the country. We had done transition year, so we were a year older than the other sixth years, and the school kept us in a separate classroom. So, anyway, the sheep carousel in Teddy's shed could fit six arses.

This is how we invented our game, me and Booly. It was called Christopher Walking. It followed the same principles as Russian roulette, but there was no gun. Here is how you play.

   1. You need seven people. The sheep carousel is the cylinder of the gun – the bit on the revolver that you spin, where the

bullet goes before it's fired. Six people must sit on the carousel.

2. One person is chosen to be the bullet, and another person is Christopher Walken.

3. If you're not the bullet and you're not Christopher Walken, you are an empty chamber. You sit in the sheep carousel, but you don't have to do anything, only sit there. There are six people in total sitting on the carousel, like the horses on a merry-go-round. And one person is not on the carousel – this person is Christopher Walken.

4. If you are Christopher Walken, you sit on a chair in front of the sheep carousel with a blindfold on, about one foot away – arm's length. You will have a rope in your hand, tied to the base of the carousel. You pull the rope hard. This will make the carousel spin, with the six people on it spinning too.

5. The Christopher Walken will wait a bit, while everyone is spinning around, and then the Christopher Walken will shout 'Fire' at their discretion.

6. If you are not Christopher Walken or the bullet, when you hear Christopher Walken say 'Fire' you put your feet on the ground so that the carousel will stop. There will be a one in six chance that the person who stops immediately in front of Christopher Walken is the bullet. If this is the case, that person (the bullet) will slap Christopher in the face, and then he's dead.

7. If Christopher Walken beats one spin, he lives, so you choose another person to also be a bullet. Keep doing this as necessary. Every time Christopher Walken lives, add another bullet – even if it means everyone on the carousel is a bullet by the end. These are the rules of Christopher Walking.

So either way, you were getting a fucking fierce slap into the face. That was the point of it. It was just a matter of when. Except if you were me.

When I was Christopher Walken, I'd never get a decent slap from any of the lads. I'd even started to edge my face forward in the seat, presenting my face to them, because they'd go easy on me. And I fucking loved being Christopher Walken. I didn't so much like being up on the carousel spinning, even if I was the bullet. I didn't get much enjoyment out of slapping someone either. I was really just waiting until it was my turn to be Christopher Walken.

Being Christopher Walken would send these electric tingles up me, starting in my feet, curling up my calves and finishing in my chest. I wouldn't let the rest of the group know this, of course. But it's why I invented the game. It was my fantasy. It was why I was obsessed with watching that *Deer Hunter* scene. When I was Christopher Walken, my hands would be shaking and my teeth jittering with this excitement. I'd salivate. I could barely hold the rope with the jitters. It would just make me feel so bold. Like I was doing something so very, very wrong, and I deserved to be slapped. The blindfold too, that was my idea. It was one of those ones you get for free on an airplane, for sleeping. I loved putting it on. The blackness of it. The feeling of being vulnerable. When it was black like that, I'd imagine a real gun pointed at my head. Mine was a gold revolver with roses etched into the barrel, a Mexican-cartel-looking thing. But most of all, I loved the tension. That beautiful moment that felt like forever after I'd shout 'Fiiiiire', and the skin on my face would tingle red, not knowing if there was a slap coming or not, and even if there wasn't, my brain would fill in the gaps with sensations, and I'd feel a phantom slap. I adored it, I lived for it. So you can imagine the utter disappointment I'd feel when all I'd get was a little tip on the cheek. Especially when the rest of the group had faces like Billy Roll from serious slaps, clatters you'd hear twenty feet away.

'I'm not hitting a girl,' Jack Foley would say to me.

And I'd say, 'Excuse me. You have my permission, Jack. I want you to slap me. The same type of slap you gave Booly last week.'

Booly would interject. 'Ah, here. My jaw wasn't right after that, Carmel. You don't want that, seriously.'

'I fucking do. Please. It's OK. I want it!' I'd roar.

'No, no fucking way. It's not on. I'm not slapping you. I don't want to do it. You'll start crying anyway.'

When Jack would say that, I'd imagine kicking him very hard in the bollocks.

'What if I do, Jack? Maybe I want to cry. But the bottom line is that this fucking game is no craic for me if ye're all getting proper slaps and I'm only getting light brushes of yer palms. Where's the fun in that? I'm the one who started talking about Russian roulette. I made the rules of Christopher Walking in the first place. I brought it to the group. This is my game,' I'd say.

And there'd be silence. Not one of the lads would hit me, while every other day they'd roar and scream like eejits, battering the heads off each other and laughing at how red they could make their faces. And I'd be jealous of their red cheeks.

'You're taking this whole thing too seriously, Carmel, and you're pulling the craic out of it,' Derek Larkin said to me.

'No, I'm not, Derek. Why can't you see it from my point of view? I just want to play the same game that all of ye are playing,' I said.

He looked at me and softened his tone down to a grandmother-type whisper so I'd stop shouting, and said, 'It's not even about how hard the slaps are, Carmel. That's not even the good part of the game. The game is about odds and seeing how far you can get without being slapped. The hardness of the slap doesn't matter to the overall game or the fun of it.'

I wanted to roll my eyes up to heaven at that comment, but Derek was the soundest of the group. He had a good heart on him, and I could tell he was trying his best to be fair. His eyes had eyelashes on them like a cow's eyes. He fluttered them down on each other and said, 'How about we all agree now that, instead of us hitting you hard, we just make a rule that none of us hits each other hard. New rule, lads, OK? Rule number eight: when the cylinder is spun, you can't hit Christopher Walken hard, just a tap. No matter who is playing Christopher Walken, everyone gets the same slap. Write it down there.'

8. Don't hit Christopher Walken too hard. No loud slaps. A pat will do.

I cringed at this. Of course it was about the strength of the slap. That was the whole point of Christopher Walking. Tension, and waiting, and not knowing, and fear, and feeling really bold, and then a fucking mighty slap in the face for feeling bold in the first place. That was the real rule, the most important rule, that I'd never write down, but that was the real rule in my head and I invented them and everyone should know this. But I agreed to go along with Derek's new rule, and I kept my mouth shut, if only to prove my point.

It was raining outside the shed, that authoritative rain that behaves like a dark grey curtain across the distance of a sky. Hammering on the roof. Violent drops.

We played again. Larkin was Christopher Walken. Booly was the bullet. The carousel spun a few times. And eventually it landed on Booly. So he leaned forward and gave Larkin a little pat on the cheek. A paltry rub, like you'd give a well-behaved dog. Under heavy rain, slaps need to compete with the noise of the torrent on the corrugated steel above. You could not hear the slap that Larkin got. There was no audible reaction from the group either, just the awkward silence of deafening rain on steel. Cotter mustered up a performative laugh, and then the rest laughed along, but they were faking it. For me, to entertain me. And we all knew the game was ruined with the new slapping rule, but didn't say it. I felt sick.

We continued playing Christopher Walking for about an hour until Jack says, 'Ah, we're always playing this, it's getting repetitive. Every day now after school. It's getting boring. Let's do something new.'

I fucking seethed.

'Oh really, repetitive ya? Nothing to do with the ould pissy slaps, no? Ha. I was right.'

Jack had a glint of contempt on his mouth when I said that. And now he wasn't even acknowledging that the soft slaps were the reason it had become boring. My forehead became very hot. Without any sense of purpose, just sheer frustration, I began slapping the shit out of my own face and head and staring at the lads while I did it, so they could see that I could take proper slaps. And that incident was the end of Christopher Walking.

Until a few weeks later.

They thought I was getting a grind for maths, but my tutor rang in sick. So I walked up through the scutters bog to where Teddy's house is. And I heard the hard slaps, and the laughter coming from the shed. And I found them all playing Christopher Walking without me. There was a clench under my bellybutton and I had to catch a breath. It hurt so much. I was tiny. I didn't matter. I was an inconvenience. The anti-craic. So I confronted them.

'It's more craic without a girl,' they said.

'I invented the game,' I said.

'We're sorry,' they said.

'Don't get emotional,' they said.

Through the hurt and rejection, I snapped. I called them all snakes and sissy boys, not fit for girlfriends. The laughing stock of the girls' toilets in school. They weren't – I hated saying that – but I was hurt and I wanted to hurt them back. Jack, in particular, didn't like this. I didn't know that this comment was a trigger for him, but I guess it was, because he had this new look on his face that I hadn't seen before. So he says, 'How about this, Carmel? Here's how we can all play. When you're Christopher Walken, instead of getting a slap, you give a blowjob to the bullet?' This was a step too fucking far. I was their friend. I was one of them.

'Ah now, Jack, don't speak to her like that. Don't be a prick – leave her alone,' said Cotter.

'No, Cotter,' I said. 'It's grand. I can take it.'

So I turned to Jack and said, 'What would you know about blowjobs anyway, you scrawny virgin? If you're such a big man, then let's play Christopher Walking for real.'

The lads went quiet. Jack just stood there, with that look, but not saying anything because he didn't know what I meant. I picked up the claw hammer with the chewed handle that was over by the tools, and I stared directly at Jack.

'You're Christopher Walken, and I'm the bullet with this

hammer. Will you play or are you a big virgin? Are you a real man or a little sissy boy?'

'I'm not a fucking virgin,' he said.

'Play Christopher Walking with the hammer then and prove it,' I said.

'Only if it's one spin,' said Jack.

'That works for me,' I said.

Derek interrupted, trying to be reasonable. 'Lads. Be realistic here – this isn't cool at all. Carmel, put down the hammer.'

I probably should have listened, but the anger wouldn't let me hear him.

Jack placed his hand on Derek's shoulder. 'Fuck her. I'm not scared. I'm not letting some bitch talk to me like that. I've a one in six chance – I fancy those odds. Even if she lands on me, she won't do it anyway.'

So he got into the chair with the blindfold on. And I had the claw hammer in both my hands, raised high above my head. And he spun us.